EVERYMAN, I will go with thee,
and be thy guide,
In thy most need to go by thy side

JOSEPH ROTH

Joseph Roth was born in Brody, Galicia, in 1894, the only son of Jewish parents. He served as a soldier in the Austro-Hungarian army during World War I and afterwards practised as a journalist in Vienna, Berlin and other European cities. After leaving Germany in 1933 he lived mostly in France and died in Paris in 1939.

Roth's reputation as a writer has grown steadily since his premature death. His novels have been translated into many languages and his collected writings, recently reissued by his German publishers Kiepenheuer and Witsch in four volumes of novels, stories and essays, have placed him firmly among the great prose writers in the German language.

JOSEPH ROTH

Weights and Measures

Translated by David Le Vay

Introduction by Beatrice Musgrave

Dent: London and Melbourne
EVERYMAN'S LIBRARY

First published in Great Britain 1982 by Peter Owen Ltd
Copyright 1934 by Querido Verlag N.V. Amsterdam
© 1977 by Verlag Allert de Lange Amsterdam and Verlag
Kiepenheuer and Witsch Köln
Translation © Peter Owen Ltd 1982
Introduction © J.M. Dent & Sons Ltd 1983
All rights reserved

Made in Great Britain by
Guernsey Press Co. Ltd, Guernsey, C.I., for
J.M. Dent & Sons Ltd
Aldine House, 33 Welbeck Street, London W1M 8LX

First published in Everyman Paperback 1983

No 1331 Paperback ISBN 0 460 01331 9

Introduction

'Joseph Roth was one of the really great writers of our day; his German prose has always been a model of perfect style. He wrote every page of his books with the fervour of a true poet; like a goldsmith he polished and repolished every sentence till the rhythm was perfect and the colour brilliant. His artistic conscience was as inexorable as his heart was passionate and tender. A whole generation loses with him a great example, and his friends a wonderful friend.' This was Stefan Zweig's tribute to Roth after his death in Paris on 27 May 1939.

Roth had collapsed only a few days earlier in the cafe of the small hotel in the rue de Tournon which had been his home for the final two years of his life. His death, at the early age of forty-four, was hastened by chronic alcoholism and an almost self-destructive neglect of his health, which had never been good. Drink had been his escape from unhappiness for many years. Since his youth he had suffered from feelings of insecurity and rootlessness, heightened by his nomadic life as a journalist. His marriage in 1922 – to Friedl Reichler, a young Viennese girl – was cut short when she developed schizophrenia in 1928 and had to spend the rest of her life in institutions (she died in 1940). Roth was haunted by guilt for her illness. He lived with a number of other women, among them the exotic Andrea Manga Bell, a half-negress, but his relationships were usually unsatisfactory as he was plagued by jealousy and hated the restrictions of domestic life. He was always short of money and died destitute. Towards the end of his life he also became increasingly depressed and anxious about the future of Europe.

Yet there was a lighter, almost childish and playful side to Roth's nature, which set off the melancholy and attracted people to him. His cafe table, where he would sit drinking and writing until the early hours – a slight figure with bulging blue eyes and a bushy moustache – was a regular meeting place for friends, passing visitors, writers and journalists, whom he would delight with his witty conversation, laced with anecdotes and *bons mots*. Roth was a born raconteur whose delight in fanciful invention included even the details of his own life. It was left to his biographer* finally to unravel the facts of his life from his fictions.

*

Joseph Roth was born on 2 September 1894 in Brody, a small town close to the Polish-Russian border in Galicia, then a province of the eastern part of the Austro-Hungarian Empire. His parents, both Jewish, had lived together for only about eighteen months when Nachum Roth took his wife, Maria, on an abortive business trip in the course of which he disappeared. He was later found to be of unsound mind and committed to the care of rabbis. His wife returned to her father's house in Brody where their son, Moses Joseph, was born a few months later. Roth never met his father.

In later years, after he had moved to the West, Roth surrounded the circumstances of his birth and early years with a web of invention. He changed his birthplace to Swaby, a tiny village near Brody, because the name in its German form, Schwabendorf, sounded more acceptable. He described his father, a small-time dealer in grain and wood, variously as a high-ranking Austrian official, an officer in the Imperial army, a Polish count, a painter – and himself as his illegitimate son. His lifelong need to embroider reality, to blur the boundaries between fact and fiction, to invent for the sake of entertaining his audience but also in order to forget what was embarrassing or

* David Bronsen, *Joseph Roth: Eine Biographie*, Kiepenheuer and Witsch, Cologne, 1974.

painful, begins with his ambivalent feelings about his childhood. Even at the time of his death his friends did not know whether he was still a Jew or had been converted to Catholicism and few of them realized that the former revolutionary, who had become an ardent supporter of the Habsburgs in his later years, had never really been an officer in the Imperial army. He told stories of having been abandoned or maltreated at birth and of spending his childhood in poverty. In reality he was brought up in relative comfort in his grandfather's house, attended elementary and high school with distinction and moved to Vienna in 1913 to continue his studies at the University there. Several of his mother's five brothers were well-to-do businessmen who supported their sister and the young Roth. But one knows from Friedrich Kargan's story in *The Silent Prophet* how much Roth must have disliked his dependence. Once settled in Vienna he tried to stand on his own feet, living on very little and eking out his income with private coaching and occasional journalism.

In the early years of the war a number of his poems, essays and a short story were accepted for publication in *Österreichs Illustrierte Zeitung*. In 1916 Roth volunteered for the army and was sent to Galicia, attached to an infantry regiment. There he seems to have worked as a press officer close to the front, seeing enough action to furnish him with first-hand knowledge about the horrors of war. His flight across the Carpathians and possible Russian captivity were other experiences that were later to stand him in good stead as a writer.

After 1919 Roth began to establish himself as a serious journalist, working in Vienna and later in Berlin and Prague. In 1923 his first novel, *Das Spinnennetz*, was serialized in the Vienna *Arbeiter-Zeitung*. In the same year he began his long association with the *Frankfurter Zeitung*: this lasted, with brief interruptions, until 1932. During this period he travelled widely – inside Germany and to Paris, the south of France, Russia, Poland and Italy – contributing essays, criticism, stories, political commentaries and travel reports also to a number of other papers, and becoming one of the most highly paid feuilletonists in Europe. In 1933, after Hitler's rise to power, he went into exile, living mostly in hotels in Paris and the south of France, with brief stays in Holland and Belgium. He continued to write novels and stories and contributed to French literary magazines and Austrian émigré journals.

In the fifteen years between 1923 and 1939 Roth produced fifteen novels which establish him firmly as one of the outstanding prose writers of his time, with an exceptional gift for storytelling. His novels are not all of the same consistently high quality that marks his best work, but they are always entertaining and told in Roth's distinctive and original style. His earliest, *Das Spinnennetz* (1923), takes as its subject the decadence of post-war Western society, a soil in which extreme ideologies like Nazism take root and where the individual becomes crushed or develops into a monster. The fate of the helpless individual, at odds with his time, remains one of Roth's basic concerns; it is a theme to which he returns in many of his later novels, finding new forms in which to express it.

His style, formed early and perfected over the years to become more expressive, varied and flexible, also remains remarkably constant. It is the product of a journalist's sharp eye, a shrewd and humorous mind, and a poet's imagination. Roth delights in significant, often quirky detail and in images of strongly visual content. Occasionally the analogies which he so readily produces give one a sense of *déjà vu*, but they enliven his prose. Irony is used to express indignation as well as pity.

Over the years there is however a noticeable change in Roth's approach as his interests broaden and the storyteller develops his full powers. In the twenties, when his themes are still closely linked with topical events, he maintains the stance of objective observer, reporting events as he sees them. *Flight without End* (1927) is an example of this manner, a product of his brief alliance with the New Objectivity: here the narrator pledges himself to report only observed fact and to invent nothing. But Roth's lively response to the world could not be contained within such rigid constraints. *Job* (1930) marks a new departure. The documentary form now gives way to fable; time becomes less specific and more distant, and the individual as the product of his age is replaced by a more universal figure. There is more room for the imaginative reconstruction of reality and for the accommodation of feeling. Personal experience has always been allowed freely into Roth's fiction, but whereas in novels like *Flight without End* and *The Silent Prophet* the autobiographical element is only thinly disguised, it becomes absorbed at different levels in the later works. *The Radetzkymarch* (1932), where the fate of three individual members of a family is set against a broad sweep of history, shows how greatly Roth has expanded his range in a decade, producing a resonant and multi-levelled work in which experienced and imagined reality are perfectly blended. From now on Roth experiments more widely with his subject matter and form, going further afield for his choice of sources and using the historical and semi-documentary modes as well as fairy-tale and fable.

Weights and Measures (*Das falsche Gewicht*, 1937), is one of the finest and artistically most satisfying examples from Roth's later period. It is a fable, set entirely in the remote border region close to Russia which contributed to Roth's earliest memories. He had introduced this corner of the empire, with its traders – many of them Jews – smugglers and deserters in earlier novels, but it had never formed the scene of the entire action. This background of an enclosed and separate world gives the novel a satisfying unity. Against it he tells his story of the just Inspector adrift in a hostile world that will ultimately destroy him, a familiar theme close to Roth's heart and one that allowed him to express something of his personal conflicts at the time. He was then living in Ostend, trying to make a painful break with his mistress Andrea Manga Bell, drinking heavily and filled with guilt and remorse. To his translator, Blanche Gidon, he wrote in September 1936: 'Je travaille, mon roman sera bon, je crois, plus parfait que ma vie.' Roth's optimism was justified; *Weights and Measures* is a vigorously told tale that shows Roth at the height of his powers as a storyteller.

His choice of setting – the Brody/Swaby district for which he felt both affection and dislike – gives rise to some of his finest descriptions of nature. Landscape and natural phenomena are evoked in memorable images that match the prevailing mood. Roth has become a master at conveying atmosphere and emotion through external events, like the changing weather or the passing seasons. From his intimate knowledge of the country, too, spring some of his liveliest characters, real in the additional sense of having formed part of Roth's imagination for years. The wily Kapturak, Sergeant Slama (who tells his own story from *The Radetzkymarch*), Mendel Singer, Sameshkin and Onufrij have all appeared in earlier novels; they are joined here by Nissen Piczenik, Roth's uncle by marriage, who is to appear once again in a later story. All are given appropriate new roles, and the incidents in which they figure are among the liveliest Roth has written – hard to match for pace and comic invention. They also have an earthy reality that links them with real experience. Many, like the raiding of Mendel Singer's shop or the arrest of old mother Czackes, seem to spring straight from the Galician soil, heightened by Roth's inventive powers and his merciless observation of physical detail.

Mother Czackes is more immediately lifelike than the two principal women, Euphemia and Regina, who play a more significant part in the action: as opposite poles between whom the helpless Inspector moves like a shuttle. But Roth has some difficulty in animating them and they remain largely types, composites standing for the archetypal figures of elusive mistress and dominant wife. The exotic gipsy, with all the allure of foreign parts, and the fickle petty-bourgeois wife have been used by Roth before. Of the two Regina has perhaps more substance. In her lilac nightgown, with her virulent green knitting and her illegitimate child, she conveys all Roth's intense dislike of confining womanhood and his feelings about loveless marriages. But she also finally draws his pity. Euphemia remains a shadow, symbol of his longing for escape, and a fixed image in the Inspector's heart. Her tinkling earrings and many-pleated skirts are picturesque details that signify her presence, but she remains largely absent. Roth's ideal women often remain shadowy, elusive like the swallows who flutter past the long-serving non-commissioned officers earlier in the book.

But with Anselm Eibenschütz, his central character, Roth has created one of his most solid and convincing figures, well delineated from without and deeply felt as the good man at odds with himself and the world. Roth can identify with his loneliness, boredom with domestic life, jealousy, melancholy and recourse to alcohol; he also shares his love of justice and feelings of despair with a world in which evil prospers. Yet Eibenschütz is defined as an individual through distance as well as empathy. Unlike Roth himself he is neither clever nor articulate, and his mute suffering is given an added poignancy by being expressed for him by his author. Eibenschütz lacks the quality of shrewdness, which Roth attributed to himself and which he clearly saw as a prerequisite for survival. In this novel the negative aspect of this quality is given to the villains – Jadlowker and Kapturak – where it is manifested as cunning and malice. Roth does not avoid the problem of evil but he does not depict it as absolute: the villains are black but they are also comical. The monsters have become more human over the years.

The exploration of evil, justice and suffering, which forms the underlying theme of *Weights and Measures*, causes Roth to ask once again 'Who really rules over the world?' – Jewish or Catholic God, or blind fate. He has asked this question many times, both in his life and in his novels, without ever finding an answer that satisfied him. Certainly the Great Inspector who appears at the end of the book is only a mechanical device, much like the God that spirited Andreas Pum out of this world in *Die Rebellion*. He speaks in riddles and supplies equivocal answers, which only mirror Roth's own uncertainties. Roth was never good at committing himself, and many of his novels have weak or ambiguous endings. Probing for causes or drawing final conclusions was not in keeping with his own contradictory and versatile nature. He himself preferred to remain elusive, leaving the reader to search for meaning between the lines. In *Weights and Measures* the last few lines are more significant than the spurious judgment. The ice over the Struminka has broken, the larks are trilling and the gipsy Sameshkin, untouched by tragedy, goes on his way once more. Justice may or may not be done but another year has begun. In the end Roth's response to life in all its variety balances the sadness and the pessimism. As a storyteller he says yes to life.

1983   Beatrice Musgrave

Novels by Joseph Roth

IN THE ORIGINAL

1923 *Das Spinnennetz* (in serial form; published 1967)
1924 *Hotel Savoy*
1924 *Die Rebellion*
1927 *Die Flucht ohne Ende*
1928 *Zipper und sein Vater*
1929 *Rechts und Links*
1929 *Der stumme Prophet* (fragment; published complete 1966)
1930 *Hiob: Roman eines einfachen Mannes*
1932 *Radetzkymarsch*
1934 *Tarabas, ein Gast auf dieser Erde*
1935 *Die hundert Tage*
1936 *Beichte eines Mörders, erzählt in einer Nacht*
1937 *Das falsche Gewicht: Die Geschichte eines Eichmeisters*
1938 *Die Kapuzinergruft*
1939 *Die Geschichte von der 1002. Nacht*

IN ENGLISH TRANSLATION

Job. The story of a simple man (Hiob)
Transl. by Dorothy Thompson. New York, Viking Press, 1931.
    Oxford, East and West Library, 1945. New York, Over-
    look Press, 1983. London, Chatto and Windus, 1983.

Radetzky March (Radetzkymarsch)
Transl. by Geoffrey Dunlop. New York, Viking Press, 1933.
    London, Heinemann, 1934.

The Radetzkymarch
Revised translation, based on the above, by Eva Tucker.
London, Allen Lane, 1974.

Tarabas. A guest on earth (Tarabas)
New York, Viking Press, 1934. London, Toronto, Heinemann,
1935.

The Story of the Hundred Days (Die hundert Tage)
Transl. by Moray Firth. London, Toronto, Heinemann, 1936.
As *The Ballad of the Hundred Days*, New York, Viking Press,
1936.

Confession of a Murder, told in one night (Beichte eines Mörders)
Transl. by Desmond I. Vesey. London, Robert Hale, 1938.

Flight without End (Die Flucht ohne Ende)
Transl. by David Le Vay in collaboration with Beatrice Mus-
grave. London, Peter Owen, 1977. New York, Overlook
Press, 1977.

The Silent Prophet (Der stumme Prophet)
Transl. by David Le Vay. London, Peter Owen, 1979. New
York, Overlook Press, 1980.

Weights and Measures (Das falsche Gewicht)
Transl. by David Le Vay. London, Peter Owen, 1982.

1

Once upon a time in the District of Zlotogrod there lived an Inspector of Weights and Measures whose name was Anselm Eibenschütz. His duty consisted of checking the weights and measures of the tradesmen in the entire district. So, at specified intervals, Eibenschütz went from shop to shop and investigated the yardsticks and the scales and the weights. He was accompanied by a sergeant of gendarmerie in full panoply. Thus the State made manifest its intention to use arms, if necessary, to punish cheats, in accordance with the commandment proclaimed in the Holy Scriptures, which considers a cheat to be the same as a thief. . . .

As for Zlotogrod, it was a pretty extensive district. It included four largish villages, two important market centres and finally the little town of Zlotogrod itself.

For his official business the Inspector used an official, one-horse, two-wheeled gig, together with a grey horse for whose upkeep Eibenschütz was personally responsible.

The grey was of a dignified disposition. It had spent three years in the army service corps and had only been transferred to the civil authorities because of a sudden blindness of the left eye which even the veterinary surgeon had been unable to account for. All in all, it was a stately grey, harnessed to a nimble golden-yellow gig. In it, on many a day, beside Inspector Eibenschütz, sat the sergeant of gendarmerie, Wenzel Slama. On his sand-coloured helmet glittered the golden spike and the imperial double eagle. Between his knees projected his rifle with fixed bayonet atop. The Inspector held reins and whip in his hand. His fair, soft moustache, assiduously waxed in an upward curve, gleamed with the same golden hue as the double eagle and the spiked helmet. It seemed to be made from the same material. From time to time the whip cracked gaily, as if it were actually laughing. The grey galloped along with haughty elegance and with the dash of an active cavalry horse. And on hot summer days, when the streets and roads of the Zlotogrod District were quite dry and almost thirsty, there arose an enormous golden-grey swirl of dust which enveloped the grey, the gig, the sergeant and the Inspector. In winter, however, Anselm Eibenschütz had at his disposal a small two-seater sleigh. The grey galloped with the same elegance in winter as in summer. It was no longer a golden-grey swirl of dust but a silver flurry of snow that shrouded the sergeant, the Inspector and the sleigh in invisibility, and the grey most of all for he was almost as white as the snow.

Anselm Eibenschütz, our Inspector of Weights and Measures, was a very imposing man. He was an old soldier. He had spent his twelve years as a long-serving

8

non-commissioned officer in the Eleventh Artillery Regiment. He had, one might say, risen from the ranks. He had been an honest soldier. And he would never have abandoned the military if his wife, in her rigorous, even inflexible, manner, had not compelled him to do so.

He had married, as almost all long-serving non-commissioned officers are in the habit of doing. Ah, they are lonely, the long-serving non-commissioned officers! They see only men, nothing but men! The women they encounter flutter past them like swallows. They marry, the non-commissioned officers, to keep hold of at least one single swallow, as it were.

Thus the long-serving gunner Eibenschütz had married, too – an indifferent woman, as anyone might have seen. It grieved him to give up his uniform. He had no liking for civilian clothes, he felt rather like a snail constrained to abandon the house which it has built out of its own saliva, that is to say out of its own flesh and blood, a quarter of a snail's life long. But much the same happened to other comrades. The majority had wives: from error, from loneliness, from love – who is to say which! All obeyed their wives: from fear and from chivalry and from habit and from dread of loneliness – who is to say which! But, in a word, Eibenschütz left the army. He doffed his uniform, his cherished uniform; he abandoned the barracks, the cherished barracks.

Every long-serving non-commissioned officer is entitled to a position. Eibenschütz, who came from the small Moravian town of Nikolsburg, had for long endeavoured to return to his homeland as a bailiff or a lawyer's clerk since he was, thanks to his wife, compelled to leave the army, his second and perhaps his actual Nikolsburg. But at that time neither bailiffs nor lawyer's clerks were needed anywhere in Moravia. All Eibenschütz's applications were turned down.

Then, for the first time, he was seized with a real rage against his wife. And he, an artilleryman who had endured so many manoeuvres and superiors, made a solemn resolve that, from then on, he would be firm towards his wife; her name was Regina. She had fallen in love with him one day in his uniform – five years ago to be exact. Now, after she had seen and possessed him on many a night, naked and without uniform, she demanded of him civilian clothes, and a position, and a home and children and grandchildren, and the Lord knows what else!

But rage was of no avail to Anselm Eibenschütz after he had received the news that the post of an Inspector of Weights and Measures was going in Zlotogrod.

He demobilized. He abandoned the barracks, his uniform, his comrades and friends.

He travelled to Zlotogrod.

2

The Zlotogrod District lay in the remote eastern part of the monarchy, a region in which there had previously been a worthless Inspector. A long time ago – the older ones could still remember it – there had been real weights and measures! Now there were only scales. Only scales. Cloth was measured with the arm, and as all the world knows, a man's arm, from his closed fist to his elbow, measures an ell, no more and no less. Moreover, all the world knew that a silver candlestick weighed a pound and twenty grams, and a brass candlestick about two pounds. Indeed, in those parts, there were many folk who really had no use for weights and measures. They weighed in the hand and measured with the eye. It was not a propitious district for a public Inspector of Weights and Measures.

As has been said, there had been another Inspector in the Zlotogrod District before the arrival of the artillery-man Anselm Eibenschütz. An Inspector of a kind! Old and infirm and addicted to alcohol, he had never checked the weights and measures in the little town of Zlotogrod itself, still less in the villages and market-places that belonged to the district. That is why, when the time came for him to be buried, he had an extraordinarily fine funeral. All the merchants followed his coffin: those who weighed with false weights, that is with the silver and brass candlesticks, those who measured with the arm, from closed fist to elbow, and many others who bitterly bewailed, without self-interest

11

and merely as it were on principle, that an Inspector of Weights had passed away who could hardly have possessed any kind of weight himself. For the people of this district regarded all those who made inflexible reference to law, statute, justice and the State as born enemies. To keep the prescribed weights and measures in their shops was as much as they could reconcile with their conscience. What, then, were they to make of the arrival of a new and conscientious Inspector? The suspicion with which Anselm Eibenschütz was welcomed in Zlotogrod matched the grief with which the old Inspector had been borne to the grave.

For it was evident at the first glance that he was neither old, nor infirm, nor given to drink, but, on the contrary, imposing, forceful and honest: above all, too honest.

3

Under such unfavourable circumstances Anselm Eiben-schütz took up his new post in the Zlotogrod District. He arrived in spring, on one of the last days of March. In the Bosnian barracks of artilleryman Eibenschütz the squirrels had already begun to glow softly, and so had the laburnum; the blackbirds were already fluting on the lawn, the larks already trilling in the air. When

Eibenschütz arrived in northern Zlotogrod the thick white snow still lay in the streets and sharp, pitiless icicles hung from the eaves. For the first few days Eibenschütz went about like one who has suddenly been struck deaf. True, he understood the language of the country, but what mattered was to understand not so much what the people said as what the land itself uttered. And the land spoke a terrifying language: it spoke of snow, darkness, cold and icicles, even though the calendar said it was spring and the violets in the woods of the Bosnian garrison at Sipolje had long since been in bloom. But here in Zlotogrod the crows cawed in the bare pastures and in the chestnut trees. They hung on the bare stripped branches in clusters, not like birds at all but like a kind of winged fruit. The little river – it was called the Struminka – still slept under a heavy sheet of ice and the children skated merrily over it, and their merriment made the poor Inspector feel even more melancholy.

Suddenly, in the night, when midnight had not yet struck from the church tower, Eibenschütz heard a great cracking as the icy sheet split open. Although, as stated, it was the middle of the night, all at once the icicles on the eaves began to melt and the drops fell hard onto the wooden pavement. A soft sweet wind from the south, a nocturnal brother of the sun, had induced them to melt. Windows opened in every cottage, people appeared at the windows, many even left their houses. In a bright blue shining sky stood the gold and silver stars – cold, eternal, brilliant, as if, from above, they too

13

were listening to the cracking and rumbling. Many of the inhabitants dressed hurriedly, as one does when a fire breaks out, and made for the river. With storm lanterns and lamps they stationed themselves on the banks and watched as the ice burst and the river awoke from its winter sleep. Some, like playful children, hopped on to one of the large drifting floes, floated rapidly downstream and, lantern in hand, signalled with it to those remaining on the bank before, eventually, alighting on the bank again. All behaved exuberantly and foolishly. For the first time since his arrival the Inspector began to talk with various inhabitants of the little town. They asked the Inspector whence he came and what he intended to do there. He replied, friendly and contented.

He stayed awake the whole night, together with the inhabitants of the town. In the morning, when he returned home and the cracking of the ice had already abated, he felt sad and lonely once more. For the first time he experienced with a shudder a sense of what was to come. He felt that here in Zlotogrod his destiny would be fulfilled. And, for the first time in his entire brave life he was afraid. For the first time, as he arrived home in the greying dawn and lay down on the bed, he was unable to sleep. He woke his wife, Regina. Strange thoughts came to him, he had to express them. He had really wanted to ask why man was so alone. But he was ashamed and merely said: 'Regina, now we are quite alone!'

The woman sat upright against the pillows, in a lilac

nightgown. The dawn filtered sparsely through the chinks in the shutters. The woman reminded Eibenschütz of a tulip which had begun to fade during this first spring night in Zlotogrod. 'Regina,' said Eibenschütz, 'I am afraid I should never have left the barracks!'

'Three years of barracks are quite enough for me,' said the woman, 'now let me sleep!'

And immediately she sank back into the pillows. Eibenschütz pushed open a shutter and looked out at the street. But the dawn too looked faded. Quite faded. Even the dawn looked faded.

4

All around there were children. There were children all around. The sergeant of gendarmerie Wenzel Slama had even had twins twice in succession within twenty months. The place swarmed with children. Wherever Eibenschütz turned he saw children. They played in the gutters with the dirty water. They played marbles in the dry. They played on the old benches of Zlotogrod's miserable park, a consumptive park, a moribund park. They played in rain and storm. They played ball and hoops and skittles. Wherever Inspector Eibenschütz turned he saw children, nothing but children. The district was fruitful, there was no doubt.

If only Inspector Eibenschütz had had children! Everything would have been different: at least so it seemed to him.

He was very lonely and he felt strange and homeless in his unaccustomed civilian clothes after being housed for twelve years in his dark-brown artillery uniform. He had his wife to be sure, but what was she to him? For the first time he asked himself why and to what end he had married her. And he was mightily alarmed. He was mightily alarmed because he had never really believed himself capable of alarm. It seemed to him that he had, as it were, been thrown off-course – and yet he had repeatedly and steadfastly kept to the right path! Nevertheless, faithful to soldierly discipline and from fear of fear, he devoted himself to his office and his duties. Never before, in this district, had there been an Inspector so devoted to state and statute, weights and measures.

He suddenly discovered that he did not love his wife. For now that he was alone and lonely – in the town, in the district, in his official position, among men – he desired love and intimacy at home and he saw that neither of these could be found there. Sometimes in the night he sat up in bed and contemplated his wife. In the yellowish gleam of the nightlight, which stood on top of the wardrobe and seemed to intensify the darkness by creating a kind of luminous nocturnal essence in the room, the sleeping Frau Regina seemed to Inspector Eibenschütz like a dried fruit. He sat up in bed and

16

regarded her closely. The longer he looked at her, the lonelier he felt. It was as if the mere sight of her made him lonely. She did not belong to him, to Anselm Eibenschütz, at all as she lay there, with her fine breasts and her peaceful childish face, the boldly arched eyebrows, the attractive half-open mouth and the small faint gleam of teeth between dark-red lips. Desire no longer urged him towards her as it had done in former nights. Did he still love her? Did he still desire her?

He was very lonely, was Inspector Eibenschütz. By day and by night he was lonely.

5

After he had spent four weeks in the Zlotogrod District, the sergeant, Wenzel Slama, suggested that he should join the savings-group of the older government officials. This group numbered bailiffs, legal clerks and even clerks of the courts among its members. They all played tarock and baccarat. Twice a week they gathered in the Café Bristol, the only café in the town of Zlotogrod. All the members of the group met Inspector Eibenschütz with mistrust, not only because he was a stranger and a newcomer but because they supposed him to be a thoroughly honest man who had not yet become a lost soul.

For they themselves were lost souls. They suffered themselves to be bribed and they bribed others. They defrauded God and the world and their superiors. But even the superiors in turn defrauded their higher superiors, who dwelt in the larger, more distant towns. In the group of older government officials one defrauded the other at cards; and not so much out of pure lust for gain but for the sheer pleasure of cheating. But Anselm Eibenschütz did not cheat. And what incensed his friends even more against him was not so much that he himself did not cheat but, above all, that he was indifferent to the cheating to which he fell victim. Therefore he appeared to isolate himself from the others in a deliberately hostile manner. And so he felt even more lonely in their midst.

The merchants hated him – with one single exception, of whom we shall speak later. They hated him because they feared him. When they saw him arrive in his golden-yellow gig, the gendarme at his side, they even dared to close their doors. They were well aware that they would be obliged to open their shops as soon as the gendarme had knocked three times. So they closed their doors merely to irritate Inspector Eibenschütz. For he had already reported several shopkeepers and brought them before the court.

When he came home late in the evening, soaked with perspiration in summer, half-frozen in winter, his wife awaited him with a sombre brow. How had he been able to endure living with such a total stranger for so long! It seemed to him as if he had only recently got to know her and always, the moment before he entered the house, he was afraid that she might have changed since yesterday and become another new, but equally sinister, person. Usually she sat knitting under the ring-burner, diligent, spiteful and embittered in her humility. Yet she was pretty to look at, with her smooth black cap of hair and her sulky short upper lip, which feigned a childish petulance. She merely raised her eyes, while her hands continued to knit. 'Shall we eat now?' she asked. 'Yes!' he said. She laid down her knitting, a dangerous poison-green ball of wool with two menacing needles and a half-begun scrap of stocking which actually resembled a remnant, a product not yet born and already dis-membered. Crash, crash, crash! Eibenschütz gazed at it while he heard the distressing noises his wife made in the kitchen and the strident and vulgar voice of the servant girl. Though he was hungry he wished that his wife might stay in the kitchen for as long as possible. Why were there no children in the house?

6

Several times a week he received a large batch of mail. Being a conscientious official, he classified all letters carefully. The inspectorate was housed in the local government office, in a wing of the court, in a small, darkish room. There Eibenschütz sat, behind a narrow green table, opposite a young clerk, a so-called contracts clerk, who was very fair, quite provocatively fair, and very ambitious. His name was Josef Nowak and Eibenschütz disliked him partly on account of his name. For it was exactly the same name as that of a hated schoolmate, on whose account Eibenschütz had had to leave the high school in Nikolsburg. It was on his account that he had enlisted so early in the army. It was on his account too – this, the Inspector only imagined – that he had married, and – more particularly – married this Frau Regina. The contracts clerk, of course, was not to blame for Eibenschütz's fate. He was not only provocatively fair and ambitious, but also vindictive. Behind compliant and wheedling manners he concealed a desire – but one of which Inspector Eibenschütz was well aware – to injure his superior.

Among the letters that came for the inspectorate there were also some that he had written, in a disguised hand. They were threatening and denunciatory letters. They disconcerted Inspector Eibenschütz. For his excessively cautious nature impelled him to investigate every report and to notify the gendarmerie squad of every threat. Privately, he acknowledged to himself that he was not cut out to be an official and certainly not in this district. He should have stayed in the barracks, yes, in the barracks. In the army, everything was prescribed. One received no threatening letters and no denunciations. The responsibility for everything a soldier did and for everything he neglected to do lay somewhere high above him, somewhere quite beyond him. How free and easy life in the barracks had been!

One day he took a few threatening letters home in his briefcase, although he had the feeling that he was committing an irregularity. But he felt compelled to show the letters to his wife and he could not withstand this compulsion. So he arrived for lunch, punctually, as he did only on those days on which he did not go on journeys to the villages of the district. The nearer he came to his little house, which stood on the outskirts of the town, next to that of the sergeant of gendarmerie, Slama, the hotter his anger became until, by the time he had nearly reached his own door, it had grown into a burning rage.

When he caught sight of his wife – who was, as usual, sitting by the window, busy with some virulent green knitting – there awoke in him a positive hatred which frightened even him. What do I really want of her? he asked himself. And as he could give no answer he became still angrier, and when he entered he threw the letters onto the table, which had already been laid, and said in a frighteningly soft voice – as if he were screaming soundlessly – 'There, read what you've done to me!' The woman laid down her knitting. Painstakingly, as if she herself were a government official, she opened one letter after the other. Meanwhile Inspector Eibenschütz, in hat and coat, as if prepared for instant departure, sat raging on his chair, and the more silently and conscientiously his wife read, the hotter became his rage. He observed her face. He thought he could see distinctly that his wife was assuming a hard, suffering but nevertheless malicious, expression. There were moments when she resembled her mother. He remembered his mother-in-law clearly. She lived at Sternberg, in Moravia. When he had last seen her, which was at the wedding, she had worn a grey silk dress, a kind of armour. It enclosed her shrunken and withered body up to the neck, as if to protect her from arrows and lances. She held a lorgnette in front of her eyes; when she lowered it, she resembled a knight who lets his vizor drop. His wife, too, let an invisible lorgnette, an invisible vizor, drop. After she had conscientiously read all the letters she got up and said: 'You're not afraid, are you? Or are you a bit frightened?'

She really is quite unconcerned about the dangers that threaten me, thought the Inspector. And he replied: 'You really are quite unconcerned, aren't you, about the dangers that threaten me? Why did you compel me to leave the barracks? What for? Why?'

She did not answer. She went into the kitchen and returned with two bowls of steaming soup. In silent resentment, but not without appetite, Inspector Eibenschütz ate his accustomed midday meal. It consisted of noodle soup, boiled beef and damson dumplings.

Without saying a word, he left the house and went to the office. He did not forget, however, to take the threatening letters back with him.

7

In the village of Szwaby, which belonged to the Zlotogrod District, Leibusch Jadlowker was mightier than the sergeant of gendarmerie himself. It must be made plain who Leibusch Jadlowker was: he was of unknown origin. It was rumoured that he had come from Odessa years ago and that the name he was known by was not his real one. He owned the so-called border tavern and no one even knew how it had come into his possession. The former owner, an old silver-bearded Jew, had perished in a mysterious, never-to-be-fathomed manner. He had been discovered one day, frozen, in the border forest, already half eaten away by wolves. Nobody, not even his servant Onufrij had been able to explain why and wherefore the old Jew had walked through the border forest at the height of the frost. All that was known was that he had no children, and that his nephew, Leibusch Jadlowker, was his only heir.

Rumour had it that Jadlowker had fled from Odessa because he had slain a man with a sugar-loaf. As a matter of fact it was hardly a rumour, it was almost a truth. Leibusch Jadlowker himself related the story to anyone who cared to hear it. He had – so he said – been a docker and there was an enemy among his comrades. And it was this fellow – who must have been as strong as a bear – whom Jadlowker slew one evening, after a quarrel, with one of the sugar-loaves they were unloading from a merchant ship. This was said to be the reason why he had fled across the Russian border.

Everyone believed him: that he had been a harbour worker and that he had murdered. The only thing they did not believe was his name: Leibusch Jadlowker – which is why he was known throughout the Zlotogrod District simply as 'Leibusch the Lawless.' There were enough reasons for calling him by this name. For his frontier tavern was the rendezvous of all the ne'er-do-wells and criminals. Three times a week the notorious Russian agent for the American Line dumped the deserters from the Russian army in Jadlowker's frontier tavern, to make their way from there to Holland, to Canada, and to South America.

As has been said: ne'er-do-wells and criminals frequented Jadlowker's frontier tavern; he harboured vagrants, beggars, thieves and robbers. And his cunning was such that the law could not touch him. His papers and those of his guests were always in order. The official informers, who swarmed near the frontier like flies, could report nothing detrimental, nothing immoral, about his way of life. But rumour had it that Leibusch Jadlowker was the author of all the crimes in the entire Zlotogrod District – and there were not a few of these: murder, robbery with murder and arson among them – not to speak of theft. He bartered Austrian deserters fleeing to Russia for Russians fleeing to Austria, so to speak. Those who did not pay him – so it was rumoured – he probably left to be shot by the Austrian or Russian frontier guards, as the case might be!

By mysterious means Jadlowker had not only acquired his licence for the frontier tavern, but also one for a grocery shop. And by 'groceries' he seemed to under-stand something quite special. For he sold not only flour, oats, sugar, tobacco, brandy, beer, caramels, chocolate, thread, soap, buttons and string, but he also dealt in girls and men. He manufactured false weights and sold them to the traders in the vicinity; and some even claimed that he also made counterfeit money – silver, gold and paper.

Naturally, he was the enemy of Inspector Anselm Eibenschütz. He did not really understand why and wherefore an otherwise healthy and intelligent man should pay any heed to government, law and statute. He hated Inspector Eibenschütz, not because he was an Inspector of Weights and Measures but because he was an incomprehensibly honest man. Jadlowker was squat, stocky, powerful and unscrupulous. It would not have been at all difficult for him to throw out the Inspector and the gendarme when they came to check his weights and measures. However, his sinful conscience impelled him not to do so. So he welcomed the Inspector in a very friendly fashion, temporarily suppressing, even deny-ing, his hatred. One would hardly have credited Leibusch Jadlowker – bear-strong and stocky as he was – with so much dissembling art. Nature wished him to be sly as well as strong.

Whenever Inspector Eibenschütz set foot in the inn at Szwaby, they would be serving sausage and horseradish and mead and schnapps and salted peas. The ninety-degree schnapps was forbidden by law; however, the sergeant drank it with dedicated enjoyment. Franz

Slama, the sergeant of gendarmerie, unfortunately became drunk easily. But this was really of no importance, as in any case he understood nothing at all about weights and measures. And even if he had understood something about them, there was no chance of ever catching a glimpse of the false weights and measures at Leibusch Jadlowker's. He made sure that they disappeared in good time; somehow he always heard about the Inspector's arrival a day earlier.

It was about this time that Inspector Eibenschütz registered a singular change in the demeanour of his wife Regina. She not only relinquished her delight in quarrelling, she became visibly more affectionate. He was rather frightened by this. For though he still loved her, because she formed part of his belongings, so to speak, like the new vocation to which he had so quickly become accustomed, he had long since ceased to desire her. She had indicated to him too plainly and for too long that she was indifferent to him and at times even hated him. For a long time now he had made a habit of going to sleep as soon as they climbed into bed at night, into the two beds pushed close together, and he no longer spared a glance for her naked body as she undressed before the mirror, perhaps in the hope that he might desire her still. Sometimes she asked him, standing there naked, whether he loved her. She really meant whether he found her beautiful. 'Yes, of course!' he said and yielded to sleep, not least to escape the pangs of conscience which his lie might yet produce.

Therefore the affection which was suddenly rekindled

in his wife surprised, even frightened, him. He slept with her, as in earlier years. But in the morning he felt out of sorts and kissed her almost with repugnance before he went off. She pretended to be asleep and he was well aware that it was a pretence. But it was her pretence and he still loved her. He did not tell her so.

In vain did he brood over what might have prompted such renewed passion. One day he was to discover the truth.

8

One day, among his many anonymous denunciatory letters, there was an unusual one that went as follows: 'Respected Inspector, although one of the victims of your harshness and in consequence involved in a court case, and that on account of a single ten kilo weight, I take the liberty of informing you that your wife is deceiving you in an underhand way and shamefully. And in fact with your master clerk, Herr Josef Nowak. Respectfully, your obedient X.Y.'

Anselm Eibenschütz was as slow as he was honest. Besides, he had discovered too often that many denunciations contained false assertions. He put the letter in his pocket and went home. His wife received him with affection, as she had done for some days past. She even clung a little longer with her arms around his neck. 'I have been waiting for you with a special longing today,' she said in a whisper. Arm in arm they went to the dining-table. During the meal he observed her closely and he noticed something that had obviously escaped him hitherto: on her little finger she was wearing a ring that was unfamiliar to him. He took her left hand and asked 'Where did you get that ring?' 'From my father,' she said. 'I have never worn it before.' It was a cheap ring, a man's ring, with an artificial sapphire. He asked again: 'Why have you suddenly put it on?' 'So that it might bring us luck,' she said. 'Us?' 'Both of us!' she confirmed.

Suddenly, too, he saw how she had altered. A new, large, tortoise-shell comb held the knot of her thick, dark-blue-gleaming hair together. Large golden earrings which she had not worn for a long time, earrings on which dangled tiny delicate gold discs, trembled on her earlobes. Her dark-brown countenance had recovered quite a youthful, indeed a maidenly, ruddy hue. One might say that she looked again as she had looked in the past, as a young girl, when he had first met her in Sarajevo, where her uncle, the master-at-arms, had invited her for the summer.

In the midst of these reflections, which by now had begun to frighten him, she uttered some unintelligible words, words without sense or meaning, so to say. They went: 'I should like at last to have a child.' By whom? he wanted to ask, for he naturally thought at once of the letter. But he said only: 'Why now? You have never

28

wished for one. You have always said that a daughter would have no dowry and a son would at best have to be an Inspector of Weights and Measures like myself.'

She lowered her eyes and said: 'I love you so much!'

He stood up and kissed her. Then he went to the office.

It was a fairly long way and on the way he suddenly remembered, or thought he remembered, having seen the ring with the artificial sapphire once before, a long time ago, on the hand of the clerk Josef Nowak. Deviousness and cunning were repugnant to the Inspector. Nevertheless, he now resolved to be devious and cunning.

The clerk got up as usual when the Inspector entered. With unwonted friendliness the Inspector said: 'Good day, my dear Nowak! Anything new happened?' 'Nothing new!' said Nowak, bowing. He remained standing until Eibenschütz had sat down.

Eibenschütz read his papers for a while and then said, with a glance at Nowak's hands: 'What's happened to your ring with the sapphire, then, Herr Nowak? It was a very fine ring!'

Nowak seemed not in the least embarrassed. 'I'm afraid I have had to pawn it!'

'Why, because of money problems?' asked the Inspector. Then the prudence of the fair and ambitious contracts clerk deserted him for the first time and he said: 'It's to do with a woman!'

'Yes, yes,' said the Inspector, 'when I was your age, I had affairs of the heart too.'

It was the first time that the clerk found his superior so friendly. But he did not suspect from this that he had been detected.

This time he deceived himself. For with the thoroughness which was basic to him, and which made him such an outstanding assessor of weights and measures, Eibenschütz resolved to investigate the matter carefully. It was not that his heart was involved any longer. He merely had a transient notion that his honour was injured – but even this notion derived only from his army days and from the recollection of the concepts of honour held by his superiors, the officers. It was, as stated, no more than a fleeting notion. Above all it behoved him, the man of honour, to search for the whole truth, one might say to establish and to check the weight and measure of events.

In consequence he went home quite slowly and with bowed head. And when passers-by greeted him he pretended not to see them, from fear that they might say something to him and distract him.

By the time he had almost reached his house, he had already made a quite specific, very methodical plan. And, being the kind of man he was, it follows that he would have to proceed exactly according to the plans he had figured out.

9

A week later he noticed that his wife was no longer wearing the ring with the artificial sapphire. He said nothing at all to his wife.

For a week he was silent, towards his wife and towards Josef Nowak. Then, however, he said unexpectedly to the latter: 'Have you redeemed your ring?'

'Yes,' replied the clerk. He feigned joyful satisfaction.

'There's no need to be embarrassed,' said Eibenschütz. 'I would willingly advance you the money!'

'Well, to be honest . . .' muttered the clerk – and now he feigned embarrassment rather than joy.

'But willingly, with pleasure!' said the Inspector. He gave the young man a solid five-kronen piece, negligently, as if had been a pencil or cigarette. Then he began affably: 'Between us men, tell me, Herr Nowak, where do you meet the lady in such a small town? Surely you can be seen?'

Cheered and enlivened by so much friendliness in his superior, the contracts clerk got up from his stool. Eibenschütz sat facing him, not unlike a pupil. It was late autumn and late afternoon. Two official oil-lamps, supplied by the local government office, burned gently under their benevolent green shades.

'You see, Herr Inspector,' began the clerk, 'in spring and summer it's very easy. It happens in the border forest. Ah, if I were to tell you, Herr Inspector, what women I've come across there! But you know that nowhere is silence more imperative than in these affairs.

In autumn and winter it is more difficult, for official reasons. In the whole district only the border tavern of "Lawless Leibusch" is suitable as a place of assignation for lovers. And you know yourself, Herr Inspector, that he is a very dangerous man and that I often have to deputize for you there. Official rectitude before everything, official rectitude comes first!'

'That's very fine,' said the Inspector. And he buried himself in his official papers. At six in the evening, when work was over, the Inspector said to his clerk: 'You can go! And lots of luck with the ladies!'

The clerk made a bow, which looked almost like the curtsy of a small schoolgirl, and disappeared.

The Inspector, however, remained seated for some time, alone with the two green-shaded lamps. He felt as if he could talk to them. They were like human beings, a species of living, mellow, shining humans. He held a silent dialogue with them. 'Stick to your plan,' they said to him, green and benevolent. 'Do you really think so?' he asked in return. 'Yes, we think so!' said the lamps.

Inspector Eibenschütz blew out the lamps and went home. He walked through a cold late autumnal rain which made him feel lonelier than ever, into a house where a lie was waiting for him, a lie that was more dismal than this evening, than this rain.

When he arrived, his house was in darkness for the first time. He unlocked the door. He sat down on the virulently green plush sofa in the so-called 'drawing-room' and waited in the dark. In this district one did not receive newspapers of yesterday or the day before

32

yesterday, but newspapers that were at least a week old. Eibenschütz never bought them. The world's events did not concern him at all.

The servant girl had heard him come in. She was called Jadwiga. Thick-set, complacent and maternal, she entered the darkness of the room. She announced to him while she was lighting the table-lamp – against his wishes, but he was too tired to tell her not to do so – that his wife had gone shopping and would soon be back. Also, she had left word for him to wait patiently.

He turned down the wick of the lamp, so low that the room appeared to be in almost complete darkness. He thought of his plan.

When his wife returned he got up, kissed her and told her that he had been very uneasy because he had been waiting for her so long. She had parcels in both arms. She put them down. They both sat at the table.

They ate together in an atmosphere of apparent friendliness and peace. At least, so it seemed to Frau Regina. She was amiable, almost eager to serve. From time to time she smiled at her husband. He noticed that she once again wore the ring with the false sapphire on her finger.

'You've got your ring back!' said the Inspector. 'I'm glad!'

'I believe,' said Frau Regina, bending over her plate, 'I am having a child at last!'

'At last?' said Inspector Eibenschütz. 'You've never wanted one before! Why now?'

'Now more than ever!' she said, and very carefully peeled an orange.

'I have today,' he began – while she was still bending her head over knife and fruit – 'been talking to my clerk, Josef Nowak. He is a womanizer, known throughout the district. He claims that he has had many women here, in the border forest in spring and summer, naturally he doesn't say which ones. In autumn and winter – he says – it's risky for him to visit Jadlowker's inn because he often represents me there officially.'

His wife was eating the last quarter of her orange. She did not look up. She said: 'Shocking, the women in this neighbourhood!'

'He gives them all rings!' retorted the Inspector.

She dropped the last piece of orange and looked at the ring on her left index finger. There ensued a long silence.

'That ring comes from Josef Nowak,' said the Inspector suddenly. 'I know it, I've seen it on his hand.'

Suddenly Frau Regina began to cry violently.

At the same time, still sobbing, she drew the ring off her finger, laid it before her on the table and said: 'So you know everything?' 'Yes,' he said. 'You are pregnant by him. I shall decide on what steps to take.'

He got up immediately, put on his coat and went out. He harnessed the gig and drove off to Szwaby, to Jadlowker's.

34

10

It was late at night when he arrived. And this caused some surprise. For never yet had Jadlowker seen Eibenschütz later than at noon. Also, the Inspector had never before appeared so animated and consequently so peculiar. 'What an honour!' exclaimed Jadlowker, and he capered out from behind the counter despite his considerable weight. 'What an honour!' Jadlowker chased away two villains who were sitting at a table in the corner. He spread a red and blue flowered cloth over the table and called over to the counter, without asking what the Inspector wanted: 'A quarter of mead and a plate of peas!'

A great din prevailed in Jadlowker's border tavern. Russian deserters sat there, only recently brought in by the border smuggler, Kapturak. They were still in their uniforms. Although they drank inordinate amounts of tea and schnapps and had been given large towels to hang round their shoulders to wipe away the sweat, they nevertheless looked like men suffering from the cold – so homeless did they feel already, barely an hour's distance from the frontier of their homeland. Little Kapturak – he was nicknamed 'the commission agent' – plied them with alcohol. Jadlowker gave him twenty-five per cent for each Russian deserter. The unexpected arrival of the Inspector seriously disconcerted the landlord, Jadlowker. He had actually intended to offer any deserters who wished to exchange their Russian uniforms cloth and suits which he had no licence to sell. On the one hand, then, the presence of the Inspector irritated him; on the other, it gave him pleasure. At last he had him, the stern one, under his roof at night – and night was Leibusch Jadlowker's great friend. He called to his little lady friend to come down.

He had lived with her for many years. It was said that she, too, came from Russia, from Odessa, and that she had a hand in more than one of Jadlowker's misdeeds. Her speech, her manner and her appearance showed that, like him, she came from the southern Ukraine. Her appearance was swarthy, wild and at the same time placid. She was young; that is to say, of no particular age. In reality – as no one in the neighbourhood could know – she was a gypsy and came from Jaslova in Bessarabia. Jadlowker had got hold of her one night and had kept her. Although jealous by nature, he was certain of the dark creature's love and all too certain of his own power over men and women. Many people obeyed him in that neighbourhood, on both sides of the border. Even Kapturak, the omnipotent commission agent, who sold men like cattle to travel agencies, sending emigrants to Canada, Java, Jamaica, Puerto Rico, Australia even: even Kapturak obeyed Jadlowker. He had bought most of the officials who might have been able to injure him. The only one he had not yet acquired was Inspector Eibenschütz. That was why, since Eibenschütz's arrival, he had waged a campaign against him. In Jadlowker's opinion every man had not only a weak spot but also a criminal one. He really could not believe – and how else would he have been able to live – that any man, whosoever he might be, could think and feel differently from the way that he, Jadlowker, thought and felt. He was convinced that all men who lived honestly were liars and he regarded them as mountebanks. The most outstanding mountebanks were the officials, followed by the ordinary respectable men, those without office. With all these one had to act a part and pretend to be respectable. That was Jadlowker's attitude towards the world as a whole. That, especially, was his attitude, and one which he maintained with a quite especial rigour, towards Inspector Eibenschütz.

11

The woman came. The stairs she descended ran by the side of the counter. She smoothed a path for herself through the noisy throng of deserters. That is, the path smoothed itself before her. At the far end of the taproom, by the window, opposite the stairs, sat Inspector Eibenschütz. He had caught sight of the woman when she was standing on the first tread of the stairs. And he had known immediately that she would come to him. He had never seen her before. Already, in that first moment, when he had seen her on the uppermost stair, he had felt a dryness in his throat, so much so that he seized the glass of mead and drained it at a single draught. It took a few minutes before the woman reached his table. The drunken deserters gave way before her delicate step. Slim, slender, narrow, a soft white shawl around her shoulders, which she held with her hands as if she were cold and as if this shawl could warm her, she walked steadily, with swaying hips and straight back. Her step was firm and graceful. The gentle tap of her high heels was audible for the space of a moment while the noisy men fell silent and stared at the woman. From the top step, her gaze was directed straight at Inspector Eibenschütz, as if her eyes strode before her feet.

As she approached him he felt as if he were discovering for the first time what a woman really was. Her deep blue eyes reminded him, who had never seen the sea, of the sea. Her white face kindled in him, who knew the snow very well, the vision of some fantastic, unearthly kind of snow; and her dark blue-black hair led him to think of southern nights, which he had never seen but had possibly once read or heard about. When she sat down opposite him he felt as if he were witnessing a great miracle; as if the unfamiliar sea, a remarkable snow, a strange night, were sitting down at his table. He did not even get up. He knew well enough that one stood up before women; but he did not get up before a miracle.

Yet he knew that this miracle was a human being, a woman, and he also knew that she was the mistress of Leibusch Jadlowker. Naturally, Eibenschütz too had heard all the stories of Jadlowker's mistress. He had never in his life had a definite idea of what one calls 'sin', but now he believed he knew how sin looked. It looked like this, it looked exactly like Jadlowker's mistress, the gypsy Euphemia Nikitsch.

'Euphemia Nikitsch,' she said simply, and sat down and spread out her many-pleated skirt. It rustled softly and penetratingly through the noise of the deserters.

'You're not drinking?' she asked, although she saw the freshly emptied glass of mead in front of Anselm Eibenschütz.

He did not hear her question at all. He stared at her with wide-open eyes and thought that only now had he really opened his eyes for the first time.

'You're not drinking?' she asked again, but now she seemed to be well aware that Eibenschütz was unable to reply. Whereupon she snapped her fingers loudly and vigorously. Onufrij, the houseboy, came. She ordered a bottle.

He brought a bottle of ninety-degree schnapps and a fresh bowl of dried peas. Inspector Eibenschütz drank, but not because he had any desire to do so! Far from it! He drank only because, in the few minutes the woman had been sitting there, he had sought in vain for some suitable word and he hoped that, if only he drank, the word would come to him. So he drank, and there was a great burning in his throat, and he went on to eat the salted peas, which further increased the burning. Meanwhile the woman sat opposite him, motionless. Her slender dark-brown fingers, each one of which resembled a diminutive, slender, rosy-headed, fragile and yet powerful woman, clasped the little glass. And

39

her eyes were not directed at Inspector Eibenschütz but at the water-clear schnapps. Eibenschütz saw her long, curved, silky black eyelashes, which were blacker than the woman's dress.

'I've never seen you here before!' he said suddenly, and turned red and twirled his moustache with both hands as if this could help to conceal his sudden ridiculous blush.

'And I have not seen you either,' she said – and it sounded like the voice of a nightingale. He had sometimes heard it in the years of his youth, in the woods around Nikolsburg. 'Do you come here often?'

'Sometimes on duty!' he said, and continued to twirl his soft moustache. He simply could not manage to take his hands away from his face.

'On duty?' she trilled. 'What sort of duty?'

He dropped his hands. 'I am an Inspector of Weights and Measures,' he said gravely.

'I see!' she said, emptied her glass, rose, curtseyed and went up the stairs.

Inspector Eibenschütz followed her with his eyes, followed the pleated skirt which seemed to turn a soft, gentle cartwheel on each tread of the stairs, followed the narrow shoes which appeared beneath it. The deserters had been snoring for some time. Some had laid their heads on the hard tables. Others lay under the tables, like stuffed, breathing sacks. All snored loudly and somewhat inhumanly.

He went to the counter. He wanted to pay. Behind the counter stood Leibusch Jadlowker and he said in a tone that was both threatening and friendly: 'Herr Inspector, today you are my guest! You shall not pay anything!', so that for the first time in his life his courage failed the former artilleryman Eibenschütz and he only said, 'Good night.'

He went home very slowly. He forgot that he had left his gig standing in front of the inn. However, the horse followed him as obediently as a dog, pulling the vehicle behind him.

It was already bright morning when he arrived. The plump servant girl placed tea and bread for him on the table. He pushed everything away.

He heard his wife's step. 'Good morning!' she said. She approached him, she prepared to embrace him. He immediately got up.

'From now on you will sleep in the kitchen!' he said, 'or you will leave the house!'

He was silent for a while, then he said: 'If your bed is not in the kitchen by tonight you can sleep with Nowak tomorrow night, or else outside.'

He suddenly remembered his carriage and his horse. They were waiting patiently in front of the small garden. It had long been broad daylight.

He drove to his office in the local government headquarters. And he wrote – in his own hand, very slowly, with double margin, in the clear childish calligraphic script of an imperial artilleryman – an application to the municipality requesting the transfer of the clerk Josef Nowak to a neighbouring municipality. He was not satisfied with him. He wanted someone else.

It caused him some distress to send a letter to the municipality. After all, he had been an artilleryman for twelve years and he had a claim to a real and proper government post. However, thanks to his wife, he had opted for this one (he was in fact a municipal official, although he was paid by the state).

At this moment it caused him special distress that he was not directly subordinate to the state.

He had arrived about an hour before duties began. When the clerk Nowak came in the Inspector said to him: 'You will leave this post. I am not satisfied with you. I have just put in a request for your dismissal or your transfer.'

The ambitious young man said only one word: 'But –'

'Silence!' cried Eibenschütz, as he had once roared out on the parade ground when he had still been an artilleryman.

He pretended to be engrossed in his documents. In reality, however, he was meditating on his life. Good – he thought – that will get rid of Nowak. I shall have nothing more to do with my wife. She will sleep in the kitchen. I won't throw her out, I don't want a scandal. And what else – what else? I won't go to Jadlowker's again – except on duty, that's understood. And if I should ever go there outside duty hours, then only with Sergeant Slama. No, I won't go there again except on duty. That's final.

12

It was not final. True, the clerk Nowak was transferred to Podgorce; true, Frau Eibenschütz slept in the kitchen, beside the servant girl: but the official visits to the border tavern, albeit in the company of Sergeant Slama, increased notably.

Winter came, and it was an inexorable winter. The sparrows fell from the rooftops, rather like overripe fruit which falls from the trees in early autumn. Even the crows and ravens, huddling together on the dead branches, seemed to feel the cold. On some days the thermometer registered thirty-two degrees. In such a winter it is hard for a man to be without a home. The Inspector stood alone in the great frost, like the solitary tree that stood, bare and freezing, in front of the office window in the courtyard of the district government office. A new clerk had come, an indolent, stout, good-natured youth who worked very slowly but exhaled cosiness. It was cosiest of all in the office. The door of the stove radiated a reddish light, the two lamps shone green. Even the papers rustled intimately. But what happened after Inspector Eibenschütz left the office? There he stood, in his short sheepskin coat with the Persian collar turned up high, in his tall knee-boots, beside one of the two street-lamps that burned outside the district government office. They burned with a very feeble yellow light, these night lamps, against the radiant snow in the park. Inspector Eibenschütz stood for a long time, pondering. He tried to picture to himself what he would find when he returned home. The fire would burn in the stove, the table would be laid, the ring-burner would glow, the yellow cat would crouch on the seat by the stove. His wife, red-eyed and sullen, would go into the kitchen as soon as he arrived. The servant girl, also sullen and red-eyed – for she shared the tears and sorrows of the mistress of the house – would blow her nose with a corner of her apron as, with her left hand, she set the plate before Herr Eibenschütz. Not even the cat would come up to him, as it had done in former times, and allow itself to be stroked. It too harboured enmity against Eibenschütz. Hate shone out of its yellow eyes. Despite everything, the Inspector resolved to go home. In his heavy boots he trudged resolutely through the crunching snow, through the dull night, illuminated from below by the snow. Not a living soul anywhere. No need to be afraid – ashamed for that matter – of stopping from time to time, for a short while, in front of one of the little houses and peering through the chinks of the shutters into somebody else's home. It was still early in the evening. Often those happy ones still sat there together. Sometimes they played dominoes. There were fathers, mothers, brothers, sisters, children and grandchildren in those houses. They ate and they laughed. Sometimes a child cried, but even crying was a blessed state, to be sure! Sometimes a dog barked from the yard, for it scented the peeping Eibenschütz. Even the dog's yelping had something homely, almost pleasant about it. By now Eibenschütz had come to know all the families of the little town and how they lived. Occasionally he imagined that it was good, useful, even necessary for an Inspector of Weights and Measures to discover something more intimate about the trading community. 'Personal information', he called it. He moved on. Now he had arrived in front of the house. His grey heard him approach and neighed pleasantly. A dear creature. The Inspector could not restrain himself; he went into the stable, he only wanted to stroke the horse, he was thinking of the happy times in the army, of all the horses in the rear quarters of the barracks, he still remembered all their names and also what they looked like. He had named his horse Jacob. 'Jacob!' he would call softly as he entered the stable. The horse lifted his head. He stamped two or thee times on the damp straw with his hoof. Eibenschütz went up to him just to say 'Good-night', but suddenly he turned round and said, 'Just a moment!' as if he were speaking to another human being. Then he went into the shed, and fetched the sleigh, and led the horse out, and buckled on the harness with trembling though deft fingers, and rolled the warm woollen hair blanket round the animal's belly, and tied it fast. He harnessed the grey in front of the sleigh. He buckled the bell round the horse's neck. He seated himself, took the reins in his hand and called 'Jacob!' He cast a brief malicious glance at the lighted windows of his dwelling. How he hated the three women who awaited him inside: first his wife, then the servant girl and finally the cat. 'Jacob!' he called, and the sleigh glided on its runners, crunching at first, then smoothly and still more smoothly and silently out through the gate. The grey knew the way.

The frost rushed round the Inspector's face, the frost was a silent storm and the night was as clear as glass, as crystal even. One did not see the stars for one had to watch the road, but one could feel them hard and clear above one's head, as if they too were made of ice. One could feel them so keenly that one could almost see them, although one had to watch the road. One speeded along.

Where was one speeding to behind the grey horse Jacob? The grey knew the way. He was galloping to Szwaby.

And where in Szwaby was he going? He was going to Jadlowker's border tavern. One might think that, like his master, he too was yearning for the gypsy Euphemia Nikitsch.

13

Inside Jadlowker's border tavern it was warm and good and cheerful. One drank, one played cards, one smoked. The smoke rose above the men's heads. There were no women present, and that was good. Inspector Eibenschütz would have found it hard to tolerate the presence of a woman, unless it had been that of Euphemia Nikitsch. But she did not appear. Eibenschütz was not aware at all that he had come here to see her. Only after he had taken a seat and a swallow did he begin to acknowledge to himself that he had really come here to see the woman once more. Occasionally Leibusch Jadlowker came to his table and sat down for a while, fleetingly, as a bee alights on honey, or a butterfly on a flower. The more serious Inspector Eibenschütz became – and he became increasingly serious the more he drank – the more cheerful Jadlowker seemed to him. More cheerful and more spiteful. He, Inspector Eibenschütz, was well aware that most of the informing letters came from Jadlowker's hand. Very probably, Jadlowker wanted to draw the Inspector's attention away from himself and towards others. He, Eibenschütz, knew it; he thought he knew it. Nevertheless, he suffered the landlord's fulsome friendliness with imperturbable patience, with a kind of devout meekness, even. He regarded Jadlowker's obnoxious, broad face with its fixed smirk. It was adorned with a small pointed, reddish-blond beard. One might well say 'adorned'; nothing could have disfigured it. It was pallid, with a waxen pallor. In it glowed two tiny little greenish eyes like lights that have already died down but still remain lights; or stars that the astronomers know to have been extinct for thousands of years although to us they still appear to be shining. The only living thing was the red goatee. It looked like a triangular speck of fire which springs, somewhat surprisingly, from matter long thought to be dead and extinguished.

'At your service, Herr Inspector!' said Leibusch

47

repeatedly, whenever he approached the table. It was as if, in the course of a single evening, he was repeatedly setting eyes on the Inspector for the first time. Eibenschütz sensed a certain irony in this behaviour; he was also able to see it as ironic that Jadlowker never came to his table without carrying a full bottle in his hand. Admittedly, this might well form part of the prescribed conduct of an innkeeper. But when Jadlowker who, to Eibenschütz's certain knowledge, had false weights, then asked: 'How is your gracious wife?', the Inspector thought he could bear it no longer; and, in order to bear it, he ordered more schnapps. He drank, he continued to drink, until the first light of day. For some time now the deserters had been snoring heavily and horribly under the tables and on the tables. Day had not yet dawned but there was already a hint of it in the air when the Inspector rose. Onufrij escorted him. Always, when climbing onto the sleigh, he felt relieved and depressed. When he reached the boundary of the town of Zlotogrod, a grey winter morning was already dawning. Eibenschütz did not return home. He stopped at Leider's, the barber's, for a shave and a hairwash in cold water. Then he went into Zlotogrod's only café, the Bristol. He drank a coffee and ate two croissants, which were so fresh that they still smelled of the baker's. Then he drove to the office, sat dully behind the empty table – on which, as was to be expected, no post lay as yet – and awaited the fat sluggish clerk with impatience. He went outside and, just as he was, in fur and boots, he washed his face and hands, under the fearfully cold pump that

48

stood in the courtyard of the district government office to serve the horses of the mounted gendarmerie.

On mornings such as these the Inspector thought of very little or of nothing at all. He thought that the clock on the church tower would soon strike eight and that the new clerk must arrive shortly. When at last it struck eight from the church tower, Eibenschütz went outside again to take a turn through the town. It had to be a short turn as the town was tiny. All he wanted was not to be there before the clerk. He also thought that a trip through the town and through the frost might make him not only appear but also feel like a man who has slept through the night in normal circumstances.

So he drove off, with his sleigh, through the crunching morning snow. Then he turned back. First he drove Jacob and the sleigh to the house. Then, not without a malicious glance at the still unopened shutters of his home, he went on foot to the office.

14

Even in the office he could not restrain himself from thinking of Jadlowker's mistress, of the gypsy Euphemia Nikitsch. In a strange manner his professional and personal loathing for the innkeeper mingled in him with a wondrous yearning for Frau Euphemia. Poor Inspector Eibenschütz, he did not know at all what was happening to him. It troubled, even shook, his conscience, that he was compelled to think of Jadlowker's legal transgressions as constantly, as relentlessly and as unremittingly as he found himself thinking of Euphemia's beauty. He thought of both simultaneously and with the same intensity. One did not happen without the other.

This hard winter, too, passed, and one night the ice on the Struminka river cracked once more. And, just as in the year when he had first arrived – only now, so it seemed to him, it was happening to someone greatly aged and completely transformed – he experienced, one March night, the cracking of the ice over the river and the excitement of the local inhabitants. This time, however, the irruption of spring signified something else. He felt greatly aged when he saw the year and the world renewing itself and no hope of any kind awoke in his heart as it had done in the first year of his arrival. Today, too, as in the first year of his arrival, people stood there on both banks of the river, with flares and lanterns, and jumped suddenly onto the shifting ice-floes and skipped back onto the bank. It was spring. Spring had come!

Inspector Eibenschütz, however, went home with a heavy heart. What did the spring mean to him now? What did it mean to him now? Three days later his wife was confined. In the kitchen. It was an easy birth. No sooner had the midwife been called than he arrived, the son of Josef Nowak. Inspector Eibenschütz reflected that

50

only bastards come into the world so quickly and easily.

The night during which the son of Josef Nowak was born to him, the Inspector spent in Jadlowker's tavern. And on this same evening Jadlowker's woman appeared again at his table. As on the first occasion Euphemia said: 'Aren't you drinking?' 'If you want me to drink, then I'll drink,' he replied. She snapped her fingers and the servant Onufrij came and filled the Inspector's glass to the brim.

She too demanded a glass. It was brought to her. She drank the ninety-degree schnapps at one gulp.

She brought her face close to the Inspector and he had the feeling that her ears with the large, gently clashing earrings were almost closer to him than her bright eyes. He saw her snow-white face very clearly but his ear was even more alert than his eye. He perceived quite distinctly the low, soft tinkling caused by the gentle clash of the gold coins against the hoops at the woman's ears every time she stirred. At the same time he noticed that her fingers were firm and strong and brown; strange to say, he no longer knew why he had to think of her fingers while he was looking at her ears and perceiving the tinkling of the small coins.

For a fleeting moment Leibusch Jadlowker also sat down at the table. A moment as short as the time a butterfly spends resting on a flower. An instant later he had gone. Euphemia bent over to the Inspector and whispered: 'I don't love him! I hate him!' Whereupon she leaned back and sipped at her glass. And the tinkling at her earlobes was sweet and soft.

51

Eibenschütz could endure it no longer. He caught the eye of the tapster Onufrij and paid and climbed onto his sleigh and drove home.

He could not remember whether or not he had said good-night to the woman Euphemia. It suddenly seemed very important to him.

The snow was still quite firm and the little sleigh flew along as if it were the depth of winter.

But the breeze from above was already mild and reminiscent of Easter, and when one looked up at the sky one could see that the stars standing there no longer looked quite so cold and pitiless. It felt as if they had moved a little closer to the earth. At the same time, a very benevolent, very gentle wind made itself felt.

A marked sharp sweetness was already present in the air. The grey sped along as never before and yet Eibenschütz had hardly tightened the reins. The grey tossed his head from time to time as if to see whether the stars really had come closer to the earth. He too felt that spring was near.

But it was Inspector Anselm Eibenschütz who felt it especially. While he glided towards his gloomy home, through the smooth snow, under the mild sky, he remembered that a bastard awaited him in his own home. But at heart he was very pleased about this. For even more clearly he remembered the remark Euphemia had made to him: 'I don't love him. I hate him!'

He heard the tinkling of her earrings!

15

At home the infant was crying. What a miracle! Infants cry. They don't know whether they are bastards or not. They have a right to whimper and cry. Besides, in Eibenschütz's ears the sound of Euphemia's softly tinkling earrings rose even above the loud crying of the infant. Eibenschütz no longer thought about his wife or about Josef Nowak's child.

When he entered his house the Inspector's only thought was not to encounter the midwife. That was his only worry. But he was altogether unsuccessful. She had heard and seen him arrive. And she went to meet him with her customary professional cheerfulness and reported to him everything he did not wish to know: the boy was a fine child and the mother was doing well.

Eibenschütz thanked her with rancour. The gold coins on the golden earrings were still tinkling in his memory and in his heart. He felt very insecure, very insecure indeed. At times he felt as if he were no longer a man but a house, as if he were capable of foreseeing his imminent downfall, as if he were a house or a wall: things burst and crumbled inside him and he hardly any longer felt the ground under his feet. He himself swayed, the whole house swayed, the chair on which he sat to have his breakfast also swayed. Because of the midwife he went straight to the bedroom, in which his wife Regina had again been accommodated since her confinement. He did not want a scandal. On account of the midwife.

He said 'Good morning' to his wife, hastily and spitefully, and contemplated Josef Nowak's infant, whom the midwife held out to him with professional zeal. The infant whimpered. It smelled obtrusively of mother's milk and urine. Eibenschütz thanked God that it was not his own son. He experienced a small malicious pleasure at the thought that it was the son of the hated Josef Nowak. But louder still than the malicious pleasure there rang in his ears the sound of the tinkling earrings.

In the afternoon he had to go on an official journey to Slodky with Sergeant Slama. It bored him, this official journey. Why wasn't he going to Szwaby? Euphemia's earrings tinkled softly.

Sergeant Slama came to collect him. The grey was harnessed to the gig. It was April, shortly after Easter. The bright blue sky with its delicate white clouds had a youthful air. The little wind that blew against the Inspector was downright teasing and wanton. The fields on either side of the highway were just beginning to turn a merry green and the patches of snow in the ditches were as grey as ash.

'Today or tomorrow the swallows will arrive,' said Sergeant Slama. It struck the Inspector as strange but nonetheless pleasant that the sergeant, despite the spiked helmet on his head, despite the rifle with the fixed bayonet between his knees, was talking of swallows.

'Do they arrive so late in these parts?'

'Yes,' said Sergeant Slama, 'they have a long way to come.'

And they were silent. And the gig rolled on and the little wind blew and the youthful sky with its pale blue cloudlets spanned the world.

It was Friday, a day the Inspector did not like: not because of superstition but because it was a market day throughout the district, in the entire neighbourhood. That made for a lot of work, not in the shops but in the open markets. The customers simply ran away when they saw gendarmes and officials arrive.

On this occasion, too, a great alarm arose in the market place of Slodky. When the yellow gig appeared on the outskirts of the tiny market town someone, a lad who had been posted as sentry, cried: 'They're coming! They're coming!' The women dropped the fish they had been just about to buy back into the barrels. Freshly slaughtered chickens, still bleeding, landed on the stall tables with a violent smack.

Even the live poultry seemed to take fright. Hens, geese, ducks and turkeys ran kicking, squawking, screeching, cackling, beating their wings clumsily and rapidly, through the broad muddy passage that ran between the stalls. While the merchants who really had no reason whatever to flee the authorities did so merely from folly, from hatred and mistrust and from ill-defined fear, the merchants who dared not abandon their stalls because to do so might have rendered them really suspicious, considered how to act. First they flung their weights into the middle of the street, into the silver-grey slime. It looked almost like a battle; as if they were fighting each other with their heavy weights on both sides of the market street.

The only one among the dealers who kept a cool head was Leibusch Jadlowker. True, he had no licence to sell fish in Slodky. Nevertheless, he sold fish in Slodky. Strong and sturdy, he stood beside his barrel, almost as wide as the barrel. True, he had no licence but neither did he have false weights. He knew the law: an Inspector of Weights and Measures had nothing to do with licences. Let him come if he liked. Meanwhile he observed the pike and carp which frolicked about in the barrel. Stupid fish, they probably thought they were still living in the river. They don't have much sense!

Ah, but how much sense does a poor man have, Leibusch Jadlowker for example?

Even if he knows all the statutes and all the habits and customs and temperaments of the officials, there comes a moment when an unknown paragraph may crop up, or, if not a paragraph, when an unsuspected passion may stir in an official. Officials are human too.

16

Inspector Eibenschütz too was only human. He could not forget the soft tinkling of Euphemia's earrings. Sometimes he put his hands over his ears. But the tinkling was inside his head, not outside. It was hardly bearable. If he were to inspect the market at Slodky quite quickly and perfunctorily there might still be time to drive back to Szwaby.

He drove through the devastated waste of a market. The wheels of his gig rolled briskly along over the discarded weights, and Jacob's hoofs buried themselves ever deeper in the mud. Eibenschütz stopped in the middle of the market. The traders stood stiff and silent behind the stall tables like wax figures in a waxworks. Anselm Eibenschütz went from stall to stall, the gendarme at his side. He was shown scales and weights, proper scales, proper weights. Ah, he was well aware that they were the false ones, which were never used. He checked the hallmarks, he investigated scoops, pigeon-holes, drawers, corners, hiding-places. At mother Czaczkes', the poultry-dealer's, he found seven false pound and kilo weights. He took down her name, he felt sorry for her. She was a haggard old Jewess, with reddened eyes, a firm nose and a wrinkled parchment countenance. It was really a matter for amazement that so many wrinkles could find their way onto such a thin covering of skin. He felt sorry for her, for poor mother Czaczkes. Nevertheless, he had to take down her name. Obviously her hands had been too feeble to throw away the weights in time, as the others had done.

She immediately began to cry: 'Murder! Murder! Help! Murder!' without rhyme or reason, in a hoarse voice that was reminiscent of crickets, of crows, of cackling. 'Not in the book, not in the book!' she cried, flapping her arms and tearing at the brown wig which sat on her silver-grey hair. And at once she began to fling her skinny hens and her miserable wares into the middle of the road, into the mud. 'Thieves, robbers, murderers!' she cried. 'Take all I've got! Take my life!' Then, without a break her screams turned into heartrending sobs. But, far from calming her, this seemed to provoke her to still greater vehemence. For while the tears streamed from her inflamed eyes and flowed over her haggard cheeks like rain, she continued to throw out everything that came to hand – a tea-glass, a spoon, the samovar. In vain did Inspector Eibenschütz endeavour to calm her. At last she seized the knife she used to cut up the poultry. She dashed out of her booth with the large saw-toothed knife in her hand. Her wig went awry, the true disorderly tangle of her grey locks was visible under the false brown hair, and the Inspector retreated a step, not on account of the knife but on account of the hair. The sergeant of gendarmerie, Slama, still stood motionless with shouldered rifle.

'She must be taken away!' he said. He grasped her raised hand in which the saw-knife threatened. At this moment all the dealers rushed out of their booths. A frightful outcry went up. One might have thought that the entire living world was crying out and raging against the arrest of Frau Soscha Czaczkes. Sergeant Slama did something else: he handcuffed the old woman. And so, scolding, screaming, croaking incomprehensible and meaningless curses, she went on her way to prison, between the two men, the gendarme and the Inspector.

As for the Inspector, he was greatly agitated. It had

not been his wish that a poor foolish Jewish poultry-dealer should be locked up. He himself was of Jewish stock. He still remembered his grandfather, who had worn a big beard and had died when he, Anselm, had been eight years old. He even remembered the funeral. It was a Jewish funeral. Enveloped in the white shroud, without a coffin, old grandfather Eibenschütz fell into the grave, which was very quickly filled in.

Ah, he was in a really bad spot, was Inspector Eibenschütz. He was pained, deeply pained, by his own fate. He was resolved to uphold the law. He was a man of honour, strict and yet compassionate at heart. What was he to do with this combination of compassion and strictness? At the same time there sounded in his ears the golden ringing of Frau Euphemia's little earrings.

He walked along as if he himself were manacled. Nevertheless, he still had to stop at one or two shops. Meanwhile Frau Czaczkes screamed horribly and the gendarme held her fast by the chain while Eibenschütz inspected the scales and weights at various stalls. He made his inspection quickly and hurriedly. This went against his soldierly and official conscience, but what else could he have done? The woman was screaming, the crowd of dealers looked threatening. He wanted to be speedy and yet conscientious. He wanted to be compassionate, considerate, and still the woman screamed and, what was more, there was a constant ringing in his ears: the sound of Euphemia's earrings. In the end he asked Sergeant Slama to release Frau Czaczkes. 'If you stop screaming,' said Slama to the old dealer, 'I'll let you go. Agreed?' Yes, to be sure, she agreed. They let her go. And she ran off, back down the road, her arms flapping. She resembled a crane.

Finally Eibenschütz arrived at Jadlowker's barrel. 'What are you doing here?' he asked. 'Have you got a licence to sell fish as well?' 'No,' said Jadlowker and his whole broad countenance smiled, as if some small, misshapen sun, a sun of the misshapen, was smiling. 'No,' said Jadlowker, 'I'm only standing in for a friend, my friend the fishmonger Schächer.'

'Papers?' asked the Inspector. He did not know why he had suddenly been seized with such a violent rage against poor Leibusch Jadlowker.

'You're only here to check weights!' said Jadlowker, who knew his way about the law. 'You're not entitled to ask for papers!'

'You're offering resistance!' said Inspector Eibenschütz. He did not know why he hated Leibusch Jadlowker so. He did not know why, constantly, in his heart, in his brain, everywhere, he heard the dangerous tinkling of the earrings.

At the word 'resistance' the sergeant stepped nearer. 'Where d'you come from?' he asked Jadlowker.

'I own the border tavern at Szwaby,' answered Jadlowker. 'I know that,' said Sergeant Slama. 'I've been to your inn. Now we're talking officially. No liberties: understand?'

He stood there, Sergeant Slama, in the evening sun. The sun was sending a last token of its strength across the market-place. It even gilded a cloud which hovered over the square, and at the same time it roused a dangerous sparkle in the gendarme's spiked helmet. Even his bayonet glittered.

No one knows what came over Leibusch Jadlowker at that point. He suddenly rushed at the gendarmerie sergeant, fishknife in hand. He uttered filthy oaths against the Emperor, against the State, against the Law and even against God.

Inspector Eibenschütz and Sergeant Slama finally overpowered him. This time the sergeant produced the real chains from his official pouch: excellent staunch chains.

Thus they drove the man to Zloczow, to the county jail.

There was no more talk of Szwaby. The soft tinkling of Frau Euphemia's earrings still sounded in the Inspector's ears.

17

Inspector Eibenschütz and Sergeant Slama had a great deal of very unpleasant business to attend to in Zloczow. They arrived quite exhausted by their journey. They had found it very difficult to get the wild and rather heavy Leibusch Jadlowker into the carriage, shackled though he was. The gendarme had had to fetter his feet as well. On the way Jadlowker had in turn spat into the faces of the gendarme and the Inspector. Although he sat wedged between the two men, he was stronger than either of them and he pushed his elbows against them with such force that both of them feared they would fall from the small vehicle. After three hours of such laborious journeying they finally arrived in Zloczow. Sergeant Slama whistled and two municipal policemen and another gendarme came to deal with Leibusch Jadlowker. It was already six o'clock in the evening when, panting and sweating, the party reached the district court. The magistrate was in a bad temper and had already knocked off work and wanted to go home. Nevertheless he hastily drew up a protocol. He ordered Sergeant Slama and Inspector Eibenschütz back for the following morning. They spent a sleepless night in a barn at the inn 'The Golden Crown', where all the rooms were occupied and where officials were not particularly welcome.

The next day and the day after that there were nothing but protocols, hearings and further protocols. Things were not going well for Inspector Eibenschütz, not at all well. He had the feeling that something important and serious had happened to him, but why did he feel so cast down by it? What on earth did Jadlowker have to do with him? True, one was human, one did not willingly bring misfortune on anyone! Or so Inspector Eibenschütz said to himself and so he said to Sergeant Slama. Was it not possible even now to go back on the whole affair? 'No, it's not possible,' said Slama.

What with the protocols, the examining magistrate, all the hearings and finally Jadlowker's own confession, that he had slandered God and, still worse, the state and its officials.

On the way back to Zlotogrod, while they were driving so fraternally, the Inspector and the sergeant, there stirred in Eibenschütz a faint envy towards Sergeant Slama, who so obviously accepted everything that had come his way. He knew the laws just as thoroughly as did the Inspector. He, too, must know that slandering God and insulting officials meant at least two years in the penitentiary. But why should Slama worry about that? The remarkable fact was that Slama did not worry about it.

The evening was already growing dark as they turned onto the broad highway to Zlotogrod. A gentle breeze blew towards the gig and combed the horse's mane. Just three kilometres outside Zlotogrod there was a country road which branched off to the border forest. To the border forest, that is to Szwaby, to the border tavern. The Inspector, who held the reins, slackened pace. He waited until it was quite dark, then he said: 'What do you think of driving to Szwaby? Then we could tell Euphemia what has happened to Jadlowker. It is really a matter of common humanity.'

The gendarmerie sergeant could not resist the phrase 'common humanity'. And although he wanted to see his wife again and although he had a fresh tour of duty tomorrow, he said: 'Very well, to Szwaby, then!'

Eibenschütz and Slama had just sat down at the table

when Euphemia came up to them. She remained standing, she supported herself on the table with both fists, she looked at the Inspector and the sergeant in turn and said: 'So you've done for him, then. And you still come here!' She said this very softly. She turned round and went away but immediately returned, sat down at the table, snapped her fingers and ordered a drink. By accident her knee encountered the Inspector's knee under the table. He withdrew it instantly but he also knew immediately that this would not change anything. What was done was done! Now he clearly heard the golden chinking of the earrings, there was ringing all about him and ringing in his heart as well. He said aloud: 'You're not cross with us any more! It'll mean the penitentiary for Jadlowker! But it's his own fault!' It seemed to him that, while he was saying all these things above the table, he was really two people, one above and one below the table. Above, he drank and spoke. But below, in the good darkness under the table and under the tablecloth, his yearning knee sought for renewed contact with Euphemia. He timidly extended a foot but touched the sergeant's boot instead, said 'Pardon!' and saw out of the corner of his eye how Euphemia smiled. This quite confused him but it also gave him some courage. So he said: 'We are both very sorry, Frau Euphemia. But we couldn't do otherwise. We are particularly sorry because now you're left quite on your own!'

'I don't think I shall be on my own for long,' she replied. 'At least you two will take an interest in me.' But she looked only at the Inspector.

She rose and went towards the stairs, up the stairs. Above all the tavern noises one could still hear the soft, sweet rustling of her many-pleated, wide, dark-red skirt.

It was late at night when they drove home to Zlotogrod, the Inspector and the gendarme.

On the way Slama said: 'I wouldn't mind her myself!'

'Nor I!' said Eibenschütz, and instantly regretted it.

'Haven't you had her yet, then?' asked the gendarme.

'How dare you!' said the Inspector.

'Well, and why not?' said the gendarme.

'I don't know,' said Eibenschütz.

'In any case,' wound up the gendarme, 'it's good that we're rid of him, that Jadlowker. My guess is two years!'

Eibenschütz cracked the whip out of embarrassment. The grey settled into a gallop. The gig glided softly and speedily along the moist sandy surface of the country road. The stars gleamed, immense and still. The breeze blew. The grey horse shimmered in the dark blue night in front of the Inspector's eyes.

Two years – he thought – two years of happiness are worth a life, two lives, three lives. He heard the soft tinkling.

18

In Zloczow, Jadlowker was in no way given short shrift,
as the saying goes, but, on the contrary, a very long trial.
He was accused of insulting behaviour, insults to
officialdom, forcible resistance to the civil power and,
what was worse, blasphemy. The trial lasted so long
because the magistrates of the assize court had not had
such an interesting trial for a long time. The county
courts of this region were very busy. With trifles and
trials. Someone had not paid someone else some money.
Someone else had had his face slapped. The county
courts of this region had a lot to do. There were, for
instance, certain types of men who allowed themselves
to be slapped, voluntarily and with relish. They possessed
the great art of provoking other men who, for one reason
or another, were ill disposed towards them, until they
received a slap in the face. Whereupon they went to the
local doctor. He confirmed that they had been injured,
and, sometimes, that they had lost a tooth. This was
known as a 'visum rapport'. Whereupon they sued.
They received justice and damages. And on this they
lived for years.

This is only by the way. It was after all entirely a
matter for the county courts. The assize court, however,
had almost nothing to do in this district. When a murder
or a robbery with murder did occur, it was never
brought to light by the police. But there were, in fact,
few murderers or violent robbers in this district. There
were only swindlers. And as nearly everybody was a

swindler, no one reported anyone else. The assize court therefore had so little to do that it almost envied the county court. Therefore it was pleased when it had to handle Jadlowker's case.

The most important thing was to examine a lot of witnesses. For all the market stall-holders offered themselves as witnesses. This meant that they had their return journey paid for and in addition received the witnesses' fee of one krone, thirty-six heller.

As they were under the impression that they could not obtain the full witnesses' fee if they were to say anything favourable about the accused, Jadlowker, they said only unfavourable things. Even Frau Czaczkes, who had actually been responsible for the whole case, declared that she had been treated with great kindness and consideration by Inspector Eibenschütz as well as by gendarmerie sergeant Slama.

The public prosecutor brought a charge of resistance to the civil power and of blasphemy. Inspector Eibenschütz and the sergeant of gendarmerie had confirmed this under oath.

Counsel for Jadlowker's defence, on the other hand, asked the jury to consider that an Inspector of Weights and Measures, an employee of the municipality in fact, had no right to ask Jadlowker for his licence. Furthermore, in taking it upon himself to arrest and even to fetter Jadlowker, the inspector had been guilty of assault. Thirdly and lastly, Jadlowker's blasphemy had not been aimed at God in general, God Almighty, but God in particular, namely the God of the officials: 'Your

God!' he had said.

Unfortunately it also emerged that Jadlowker had escaped from Odessa and that once, many years ago, he had slain a man with a sugar-loaf.

The testimony of Jadlowker's mistress, Fräulein Euphemia Nikitsch, did not significantly affect the progress of the trial, although it did not fail to make an impression. The solemnity of the court did not prevent her from asserting, with downright malicious friendliness, that she had always taken her friend Leibusch Jadlowker for a violent-tempered and particularly irreligious man.

Poor Jadlowker sat helplessly in the dock, between two guards. Not only did he not defend himself, it did not even occur to him that he was in any way capable of defending himself. His entire life had been ransacked. It had been discovered that he had immigrated from Russia. It had further been discovered that once, many years ago, he had killed a man in Odessa with a sugar-loaf.

However, he had killed not one man but several men and so he kept silent. Also his name was not Jadlowker but Kramrisch. He had merely appropriated the papers, and naturally also the name, of one of his victims.

He was finally sentenced to two years in the penitentiary, plus one fast-day a week, on a Friday, the day when he had committed this misdeed.

Silent and determined, he suffered himself to be led away.

19

Inspector Eibenschütz felt as if he and not Leibusch Jadlowker had been sentenced. Why this should be so he did not know, he did not know at all. He resolved never again to go to the border tavern. Nevertheless he looked around for Frau Euphemia. But she had disappeared, disappeared in a mysterious manner.

He drove home very silently with Sergeant Slama. The way was long, some thirteen kilometres. During the journey the Inspector was silent although the gendarme again and again attempted to make conversation. The trial had made Sergeant Slama extremely cheerful while it had made Inspector Eibenschütz extremely depressed.

He found himself in a strange frame of mind, did Anselm Eibenschütz: he thought of poor Jadlowker with compassion, with genuine sorrow even; at the same time, however, he could not conceal from himself the fact that the sentence of two years of penitentiary passed on Jadlowker actually made him very glad. He did not know precisely why, or, rather, he did know precisely why but did not want to admit it to himself.

He struggled with himself as to whether or not he should admit to his actual knowledge. The gendarmerie sergeant Slama seemed to talk all kinds of foolish rubbish en route. Never before - so it seemed to Eibenschütz - had Slama uttered so much foolishness.

Evening had already set in. They rolled on along the wide sandy road between two forests. They rolled in a

69

westerly direction. The setting sun, ruddy and benevolent, shone straight in their eyes and dazzled them. The pines on the edge of the forest, which lined the road on both sides, glowed as if from within, as if they had drunk the reddish gold of the sun and were now radiating it. One could hear the ceaseless piping, warbling, twittering and whistling of the birds and one smelled the sharp resinous smell, harshly sweet and astringent, that emanated from the two boundless forests. The aroma was sharp and sweet and bitter all at the same time. It excited Inspector Eibenschütz, and he stroked the grey's right flank gently with the whip to urge him on. But why urge him on? Where was he hurrying to? Home? Did he have a home? Did he still have a home? Was not a strange infant screaming in his home? Nowak's infant? Ah, how could a poor Inspector of Weights and Measures know the answers! Eibenschütz felt naked, quite naked, as if fate had stripped him bare. He was ashamed, and what was worse, he really did not know why he was ashamed. If, before, he had urged his horse on, now he endeavoured to curb his gallop. The stars were already glittering in the sky, very far away and quite enigmatic. From time to time Eibenschütz gazed up at them. He tried to find some comfort there, he sought to get closer to them, as it were. In former years he had never taken any notice of them, let alone liked them. Now, all of a sudden, he felt as if they had always played a part in his life – from afar, it was true, but a part nevertheless, rather as very distant relations sometimes do.

Now they were arriving at the town of Zlotogrod.

'Shall I put you down?' Eibenschütz asked the gendarme.

'To be sure,' said the sergeant. 'I'm tired.'

Sergeant Slama lived on the outskirts of Zlotogrod, where the road to Szwaby branched off. A white arrow on a weathered signpost indicated the road to Szwaby; the white arrow shone bright, almost dazzling, through the light-blue night.

Inspector Eibenschütz took his leave of the gendarme.

He really meant to drive home, did the Inspector. But the arrow, the arrow, shone too brightly. And so Eibenschütz turned his gig towards Szwaby, towards the border tavern.

20

Jadlowker had taken out several mortgages on the border tavern. This now emerged. Immediately after he had been sentenced the question was raised in the town of Zlotogrod, and in the district as a whole, as to who should take over the border tavern at Szwaby – only temporarily, of course, according to the official version, but in reality for good. For the border tavern was a good business and the fact that Leibusch Jadlowker owned it had long been a matter for envy. That evening, without

71

a previous appointment, the five mortgagees met together in the border tavern at Szwaby. All five arrived at almost the same time, all five were startled to meet each other there. The richest among them was Kapturak.

It was he who brought the deserters here; he really traded in them. He alone knew exactly what the dealings of the tavern brought in, for he himself owned a similar inn on the other side of the border, on Russian territory. The other mortgagees, however, were amateurs: a coral dealer named Piczenik; a fishmonger named Balaban; a cab-driver named Manes; and a seller of dairy products named Ostersetzer.

All four were far less shrewd than little Kapturak. Fräulein Euphemia Nikitsch sat at the table, she belonged to the inn, the mortgages were taken out on her too. All five mortgagees did not in fact look at her while they were negotiating, but all five were aware that she was there, that she was present and that she was listening. None of the five pleased her: not the exceedingly skinny Piczenik; not the exceedingly fat Balaban; not the driver Manes, the boor; and not Ostersetzer, because he was pockmarked and his beard was sparse and meagre like the beard of a billygoat. The one she, Euphemia, liked best was the tiny Kapturak. Though he was small and repulsive, he was more cunning and richer than the others. She sat down beside him. They drank the health of the condemned Jadlowker. All clinked their glasses.

At that moment the bell of a carriage was heard and

Euphemia knew at once that it was the Inspector's carriage. She got up. In truth, she loved him. She also loved money, security, the inn, the shop that was part of it, as well as poor Jadlowker who was now sitting in the penitentiary, but the last named only in remembrance of the good times she had enjoyed with him. For she had a grateful disposition, like so many frivolous persons. Memories generally made her melancholy and affectionate. She jumped up when she heard the Inspector's carriage.

At the same moment he entered; tall and imposing as he was, he almost seemed to obliterate all the others. His bushy, fair, vigorous moustache gleamed brighter than the three oil-lamps in the centre of the room. All five mortgagees jumped up as well. He barely greeted them. He simply sat down, conscious of his authority, and as if he sensed behind him the invisible pressure of the sergeant of gendarmerie Slama, standing with fixed bayonet and wearing the gleaming spiked helmet.

The conversation died away. Soon the mortgagees got up and left. They looked as if they had been thrashed, they put one in mind of dogs.

21

It must be said that the border tavern at Szwaby was no ordinary tavern. Even the government took an interest in it. It was obviously important for the government to know how many and which deserters arrived from Russia every day.

One day the government took an interest in one thing and the next in another. It even took an interest in Frau Czaczkes' poultry; in Balaban's weights; in Nissen Piczenik's school-age children; the government took an interest in vaccinations, in taxes, in marriages and in divorces, in wills and estates, in smuggling and in forgers. Why should it not take an interest in Jadlowker's border tavern, in which all the deserters congregated? The district authority had a political interest in seeing that the border tavern was under proper surveillance. With this in mind it turned to the municipality of Zlotogrod. And the municipality of Zlotogrod appointed Inspector Eibenschütz as provisional manager of the border tavern.

The consequence of this was that Eibenschütz experienced great pleasure and, at the same time, great embarrassment. He was pleased and did not know why. He was afraid and did not know what he feared. When he received the document marked 'Strictly confidential', in which he was charged by the municipality, at the instance of the government authorities 'to take over the supervision of the inn and related interests of the landlord and grocer Leibusch Jadlowker during his absence', he believed that fortune and misfortune had befallen him at the same time and he felt like a man who dreams that he is standing on a broad open plain, buffeted by two different kinds of wind at once, a north wind and a south wind. Bitter grief and sweet joy breathed on him simultaneously and furiously. He could of course decline the request of the municipality acting in the name of the district authority. In the letter it stated: 'It is left to you to render a report accepting or rejecting the proposal.' This made the Inspector's position even more difficult. He was not used to making decisions. He had served for twelve years. He was accustomed to obey. If only he were still in the barracks, had stayed in the army!

He went home very slowly, hat in hand and with lowered head. He had plenty of time, he imagined that the way was longer than usual. Strange to say, he felt no aversion towards his home and what it sheltered: his wife and the bastard. He had not seen the child since the evening when the midwife had brought it to him. Nor did his wife show herself in the hours when he was at home. Only occasionally he heard the child screaming behind the closed door. This gave him a certain pleasure, strange to say it did not annoy him in the least. He even smiled to himself when he heard the little one cry. If it cried, the little one, it was a sign that it was out of temper. Its mother too was out of temper, and so was the servant girl, Jadwiga. Let them all be out of temper!

This evening no sound penetrated the closed door. The servant girl Jadwiga entered without speaking, she brought in the soup and the meat at the same time – for Eibenschütz had forbidden her to come into the room twice in the course of an evening. He ate hastily and left half on his plate. He missed the child's crying and his wife's lulling song.

During the meal he drew the strictly confidential letter from his pocket and read it through once more. For a while he believed that new possibilities, new interpretations, might arise from the words, from the letters even. But after he had read the letter a couple of times he had to admit to himself that it contained nothing mysterious and no hidden meaning.

He had to make a decision, there was no doubt about it. The plates still stood before him, half-empty, pushed back and rejected. In a moment he was on his feet. He went into the shed and trundled the gig into the yard, then into the stable so that he might untie the grey horse Jacob.

He harnessed up, he drove off. He sat calmly on his seat, his hands in his lap. The reins lay loosely over the back of the old horse, the ends were twisted round the brake handle. On the left the whip leaned in its leather holder.

Without reins, without whip, without orders of any kind, the grey in due course deposited him at Szwaby right in front of the door of the border tavern.

Eibenschütz at once asked for Frau Euphemia.

He did not sit down, he considered it necessary to adopt a kind of official attitude, as if he had come here with the firm resolve to take over the management of the

76

hostelry. Official attitude – he said to himself – and he remained standing at the foot of the stairs with his hat on his head. It was some time before she came down. After a long while he heard her heel on the stair. He did not look up but he thought he could clearly picture her foot, a long narrow foot in a long narrow shoe. All at once there was the rustling sound of her many-pleated wine-red dress. Her hard, firm, even step resounded on the hard, wooden, bare treads. Eibenschütz did not want to look up. He would much rather imagine the way she walked and the way the many, many tiny pleats of her dress were moving. He would have liked the stair to have many more treads. Now she had descended, was already standing before him. He took off his hat.

He said, without exactly looking at her, speaking across her head but so that he perceived very distinctly the blue-black sheen of her hair: 'I have something special to say to you!'

'Say it then!'

'No, something very special! Not here!'

'Then let's go outside,' she said, and stepped ahead to the door.

The moon stood large and mellow over the courtyard.

The dog barked ceaselessly. The grey horse stood tied to the yard-gate, its head drooping as if deep in thought. The sweet and heady smell of acacias filled the air, and it seemed to Eibenschütz that all the scents of this spring night emanated from the woman, that she alone was able to bestow on the night the fragrance and the glitter and the moon and all the acacias in the world.

'I am here on official business today,' he said. 'I trust you, that's why I am telling you this, Euphemia,' he added after a while. 'None of the mortgagees is to be allowed into this house. I have been ordered to take charge and to supervise things. If you agree, we shall get on well together.'

'Of course,' she replied, 'why should we not get on splendidly?'

It seemed to the Inspector that her voice sounded quite different in the silvery blue of the night than in the inn parlour. The voice was loud, clear and gentle, it had, as it were, arches and curves; Eibenschütz believed he could see the voice and almost catch hold of it. Soon after, he had the sensation that it made an arch over his head and that he was standing directly beneath it.

It was only after it had died away that he grasped what the voice had said. They would get on well together. And why not?

'It's strictly confidential,' he said. 'You understand that? You won't say a word to anyone?'

'Not a word to anyone,' she said and held out her hand to him, a gleaming white hand. It looked as if it was swimming through the silver-blue night.

He waited a while, he looked at the gleaming hand for a long time before he took it. It was cold and warm at the same time, it seemed to him that the palm was hot and the back cold. He held onto the white gleaming thing for some time. When he let it go Euphemia was smiling. Her sparkling teeth showed clearly in the blue of the night.

She turned round quickly and her many-pleated skirt rustled, very softly. The dress had a life of its own, it was a kind of living, magic tent. It whispered, it rustled.

When the Inspector returned to the inn Sergeant Slama and the rogue Kapturak were sitting at a table playing tarock. Eibenschütz joined them.

'Poor fellow, that Jadlowker,' said Kapturak, 'eh, Herr Inspector?'

Eibenschütz did not answer but Sergeant Slama said impatiently: 'We'll catch you too one day, Herr Kapturak! Do you feel like another game?'

22

Most people depart this world without having acquired so much as a grain of truth about themselves. Possibly they acquire it in the next world. Some, however, are granted self-knowledge while they are still in this world. It usually comes to them quite suddenly and alarms them mightily. Inspector Eibenschütz belonged to this category of men.

Summer came suddenly, without any transition. It was hot and dry, and if now and again it brought a storm in its train, this passed quickly and left behind it a still more intense heat. Water was scarce, the springs ran dry. The grass in the meadows soon turned yellow and withered and even the birds seemed to die of thirst. They were numerous in this neighbourhood. Each summer that Eibenschütz had spent here had been filled with their fervent, clamorous singing. This summer, however, they did not show themselves much and the Inspector noticed to his astonishment that he missed their song. When had he ever cared about the song of the birds? Why, all of a sudden, was he aware of all the changes in nature? What had nature meant to him, the artilleryman Eibenschütz, in the past? Good or poor visibility. A parade ground. Whether to wear one's overcoat or carry it. Whether to move on or stay put. Whether to clean one's rifle twice a day or only once. Why did Inspector Eibenschütz suddenly feel all the changes in nature? Why was he now enjoying the deep summery green of the large, broad, rich chestnut leaves and why did the scent of the chestnuts so powerfully overwhelm his senses?

His child, that is the clerk Nowak's child, was now taken for outings in a perambulator. He sometimes encountered his wife in the small municipal park when he traversed it on his way from the office to his home. It was too hot to march over the paving-stones. When he met his wife Eibenschütz walked along with her for a while, behind the perambulator, and they did not utter a word. For a long time he had felt no hate, either towards his wife or towards the child; he was indifferent to both of them, at times he even felt compassion for both. He walked along behind the baby carriage, beside his wife, simply because he was concerned that the people in the little town should believe that all was well. Suddenly he would turn round, without a word, without a salutation, and go home. The servant girl brought him his meal. He ate hastily and absentmindedly. He was already thinking of the grey, of the gig, of the drive to Szwaby, of the border tavern.

He went outside into shed and stable, he harnessed up and drove off. He drove along in golden clouds of dust and sand, his throat was dry, the relentless sun stabbed with a thousand lances at his head through the broadbrimmed straw hat, but his heart was light. He could have stopped at many a hostelry, there were hostelries in plenty along his route. He stopped nowhere. Thirsty and hungry as his soul was, so he too wanted to arrive at Szwaby, at the border tavern.

He arrived and it took a good two hours. The grey, Jacob, was already fretting; he let his tongue hang out, he longed for water and his flanks quivered in heated agitation. The groom came to unharness him. Since Jadlowker had been locked up the groom regarded Inspector Eibenschütz as the legitimate owner of the border tavern. He was an old groom, a Ruthenian peasant. Onufrij was his name, and he was deaf to boot. One might have thought that he understood nothing but he grasped everything, possibly because he was so deaf and so old. Many who hear little are capable of noticing quite a lot.

The Inspector sat down at the table by the window. He drank mead and ate salted peas. Kapturak approached him in humble friendliness, for no other purpose than to pass the time of day. The Inspector hated this humble familiarity. Strange to say, he himself was beginning to realize that his growing sensitivity to the processes of nature also made him more sensitive to the wickedness of men. It seemed unjust to the Inspector that Jadlowker had been condemned while Kapturak was running around free. What a pity that Kapturak gave no grounds for conviction by transgression of the law. He had no open shop, no scales, no weights. One day however they would catch him nevertheless.

Eibenschütz drank for a while, then rose and ordered the barmaid to call Euphemia. He posted himself at the foot of the stairs to await the woman.

Kapturak was still bringing Russian deserters to the border tavern every day, that is to say every night. They were very profitable for they were desperate and without hope, and people who are desperate and without hope spend money. But there were also spies among them who denounced their companions in misfortune and gave all kinds of information about matters concerning conditions at the frontier. Now, to practise police surveillance in no way formed part of the duties of an Inspector of Weights and Measures, nor was it in the nature of Anselm Eibenschütz to do so. However, he paid attention and endeavoured to listen to conversations and remember faces. It was repugnant to him and yet he did it.

Euphemia was not upstairs in her room but next door in the open shop, where she sold the peasants turpentine, groats, tobacco, herrings, sprats, greaseproof and silver paper and blue dye for lime-wash. The shop was open only on two days a week, on Mondays and Thursdays. Today was Thursday. Eibenschütz waited in vain at the foot of the stairs. Euphemia took him unawares.

She gave him her hand and he remembered how this hand had come towards him, had swum towards him, through the silver-blue night in the spring a few weeks earlier. He took hold of the hand and held it for a long time, longer than he felt proper, but what was he to do?

'What do you want of me?' asked Euphemia.

He wanted to say that he had come here in the course of his official duty but instead he said: 'I wanted to see you again!'

'Come into the shop,' she replied. 'I have no time, the customers are waiting.'

He went into the shop.

The golden summer evening was already under way.

The deserters were singing in the tavern. They drank tea and schnapps and wiped the sweat from their faces after each swallow. Each of them had a towel hanging round his neck. They broke off their singing for a moment as Euphemia and the Inspector went out.

Many peasants and Jews were waiting in the little shop. They wanted turpentine, wax, Sabbath candles, emery paper, tobacco, herrings, sprats and blue distemper. Inspector Eibenschütz, who had so often come here in the course of official duty, as the executor of inflexible laws, in order to check scales and measures and weights, found himself unexpectedly behind the

83

counter beside Euphemia. And, as if he were her apprentice, she ordered him to fetch this and that, to weigh this and that, to serve this one and that one.

The Inspector obeyed. What was he to do? He was not even aware that he obeyed.

The customers left. Euphemia and the Inspector left the shop. They had barely three steps to cover to the inn. But to Eibenschütz it felt as if they needed a long, long time to do so. The good cool summer night had already begun.

23

That night he stayed very late in the border tavern, until the first light of day, until the hour when the municipal constable Arbisch came to round up the deserters. This morning, for the first time for many weeks, the sky was cloudy. The sun, red and small like an orange, rose in the sky as Eibenschütz drove out of the inn gate. The air already smelled sweet and bright and humid after the long-awaited rain. A gentle breeze wafted towards Eibenschütz. Although he had been drinking all night long, he felt fresh and almost weightless. He felt very young and it seemed to him that he had not really experienced anything until this hour, nothing at all. His life was just about to begin.

He had already been travelling for about an hour and was halfway home when the rain began to fall, softly at first, then gradually getting heavier. All around, everything breathed moist soft goodness. Everything along the route seemed to yield itself willingly to the rain. The lime trees by the road bowed their heads. The willow bushes on both sides of the passable tracks in the marsh of Zubrowka seemed to have raised themselves up, trembling voluptuously in the warm downpour. Almost at once the birds began their singing, which the Inspector had missed for so long. The blackbirds chirped the loudest. How strange – the Inspector said to himself – and unusual it was that the birds should cheep and twitter and trill in the midst of all this rain; probably – he thought further – they welcomed it as much as he did. But why should he welcome the rain? What did the rain have to do with him? I must have undergone a great change since I came to this neighbourhood! What has the rain to do with me? Why should the birds concern me?

Suddenly, he himself did not know why, he tugged at the reins and the grey stopped still. There he sat, the Inspector, on the seat with the rain streaming down on him and the white straw hat flopping on his head like a wet rag. He stopped still in the rain, instead of driving on as others would have done.

He turned around suddenly. He cracked the whip. The grey began to gallop. A bare half-hour later he was back in Szwaby. It was still raining in torrents.

Eibenschütz took a room in the hostelry. He told

Onufrij that along the way the ground had turned to mud and that no one could drive further. So he would prefer to spend the night here until the rain had stopped.

He was given a room. He slept lightly and dreamlessly and did not awake till evening.

The rain had long since stopped. The foliage on the trees outside the window was dry. The stones in the inn-yard were dry, the sun was just on the point of setting, in full splendour. The sky was cloudless.

The Inspector went into the inn parlour.

24

He waited for Euphemia, she did not come. He sat there, his head resting in his hands. He did not really know what he was doing here. Through the noise made by the other guests he heard the hard, relentless ticking of the clock on the wall. Gradually he began to believe that he had not come to this place of his own free will but that someone had brought him here. Only, he did not remember who it was; he did not know who it could have been.

The door opened, marked by a draught of air, and Kapturak entered. He went straight to the Inspector's table. 'What about a game?' he asked. 'Good, let's play.'

So he played a game of tarock, and a second and a

third. He waited in vain for Euphemia. He lost all three games.

The day too was lost, and so was the night. He did not know what to do. He did not utter a word, not even to Kapturak. He waited for Euphemia. She did not come.

Around three o'clock in the morning a deserter began to play the accordion. He played the song '*Ja lubyl tibia*' – and everyone began to cry. They cried for the homeland which they had just abandoned. At this moment they yearned more for their homeland than for freedom.

Tears stood in every eye. Only Kapturak's eyes remained dry. Even an accordion could not touch him. He was the one who brought the deserters across the border. He made his living that way. The homesickness of the deserters, their yearning for freedom, earned him his living.

Even Inspector Eibenschütz became melancholy. He listened to the melody, '*Ja lubyl tibia*', and felt his eyes grow moist. Almost at the same moment as the accordion began to play, Kapturak asked whether Eibenschütz would like to play another game. 'Yes,' said Eibenschütz, 'why not?' And they played the fourth game of tarock. Eibenschütz lost once more.

Day was already dawning when Eibenschütz rose from the table. He went up the stairs and had to hold on to the banisters with both hands.

He staggered into his room. He lay down on his bed fully clothed, as in former times during army manoeuvres. He slept dreamlessly and quite peacefully. The first chirping of birds awoke him. He rose at once and immediately he knew where he was: here, in the border tavern; this in no way puzzled him.

He had nothing to wash himself with. He could not shave. This troubled him. He felt sullied as well as despoiled. In spite of this he went downstairs.

The bright summer morning streamed vigorously through the open windows. The deserters were still asleep on the floor. Even the morning sun did not succeed in waking them, nor the loud trumpeting song of the morning blackbirds.

Right among the sleeping deserters who were lying at his feet Inspector Eibenschütz sat and drank his tea.

Onufrij served him. 'Where's Euphemia?' asked the Inspector. 'I don't know,' said Onufrij. 'I would like to see her,' said Eibenschütz, 'I've something important to tell her.'

'Good,' said Onufrij, and Eibenschütz remained seated. She soon appeared, Euphemia herself. He was embarrassed in her presence, unwashed as he was and with yesterday's growth of beard.

'I've been waiting for you all night,' he said.

'Well, you can see me now!' she replied. 'You are staying here?'

He had not fully realized that he had come here to stay. How simple it was. Of course! What was there left for him at home? 'Yes, yes,' he said, addressing himself to the early morning through the open door. The men on the floor slowly awoke. They crouched dully for a while, rubbed their eyes, and only then did they seem to notice that it was morning. They got up and, one after the other, went out into the yard to wash at the well.

Eibenschütz remained alone with Euphemia in the large bar parlour, which had suddenly grown even larger, as if all the time the dawn was enlarging it still more. It smelled of the dawn and also of the previous day, of the men's clothes and of their sleep, of brandy and mead and also of summer and of Euphemia. All these odours now assailed poor Eibenschütz. They confused him and yet he accurately marked each one.

Many things, very many things, went confusedly through his head. He grasped that he had nothing sensible left to say and yet he must do something, and Euphemia was sitting beside him. He suddenly embraced her and kissed her heartily and passionately. Then, as the men from the well approached the door, he said, simply and honestly, 'I love you!' and quickly rose to his feet. He had his horse harnessed. He drove home to fetch his things.

25

As long as the summer lasted Eibenschütz was happy. He experienced love and all the blissful changes it produces in a man. Upright and simple as he was, with a somewhat grave disposition, he experienced the first passion of his life profoundly and honestly, in all its awesome, thrilling bliss. During this time he carried out his official duties in a carefree as well as careless manner. The long summer days were only minor postscripts to the short, packed, vigorous nights. What one did by day, without Euphemia, was of no consequence.

Barely once a week did Eibenschütz go home, to his wife. He went out of a kind of sporadic sense of duty and on account of the neighbours. They all knew that he was living with Jadlowker's woman, but as he had become so mild and neglectful, they too regarded him with mild, or at least indifferent, eyes. Moreover, he did not concern himself with the task that had been entrusted to him. The hostelry and the shop were looked after by Euphemia alone, and she also took care of the papers of those who came across the frontier, and in her helpless handwriting entered the names in the big book at which the gendarmes glanced only rarely and fleetingly.

So autumn arrived. And with it, as every other autumn, came the chestnut-roaster and Sameschkin; Sameschkin, from Uchna in Bessarabia, arrived in Szwaby. He was a distant relative of Euphemia's; at all events, so she said. He was her sweetheart, that was no secret, all the world knew it. Jadlowker had got on well with him. Sameschkin always came in October. He stayed for the winter. He arrived with many sackfuls of chestnuts and with his small roasting oven on its four spindly black legs. He looked very foreign, as if he too had been roasted. The sun of Bessarabia and the

Caucasus and the Crimea had done this to him. His small quick eyes called to mind the charcoal with which he roasted his chestnuts, and his long narrow moustache, reminiscent of a finely curved switch of hair, was even blacker than the iron oven. His hands and his feet were brown as chestnuts. On his head he wore a tall fur cap of astrakhan, and round his body a white, soot-blackened and greasy sheepskin. He had large, really massive, knee-boots with very wide legs to them. In his belt was stuck a heavy stick of cherry-wood furnished below with a four-sided iron spike. Thus he was completely equipped for a hard winter and for a hard vocation.

He was a good-natured, even a soft-hearted, man. He spoke a mixture of many languages which no one in the district understood. Here he was simply called 'the gypsy', and only a few knew that his name was Sameschkin. Konstantin Sameschkin was his name. He sold twenty chestnuts for a dreier, he sold his wares by the piece. He often smiled; his teeth appeared large and white under his black moustache. They called to mind white piano keys.

There were two other chestnut-roasters in the whole district, one in Zlotogrod itself. But they were not as esteemed as Sameschkin, the gypsy. People came from all over the district to buy his chestnuts, raw and roasted. The raw ones he sold for ten pfennigs a pound.

To be sure, Eibenschütz also knew that Sameschkin was Euphemia's lover. In the past, Sameschkin had travelled through other countries and other districts with his chestnuts. Every year he had wintered in a different place. But for years now, out of plain devotion to Euphemia, he had come to Szwaby. During the summer he earned his living doing casual labour in Uchna, Bessarabia. Sometimes he helped the wood-cutters, other times the charcoal-burners, sometimes he dug wells, sometimes he cleared out cesspits. He had never yet seen a town larger than Kishinev. Inoffensive as he was, he believed that Euphemia was true to him. During the summer he told anyone who would listen that each autumn he went to see his wife, that she was employed in the border tavern at Szwaby and could not always accompany him. He anticipated the autumn as keenly as others do the spring.

It did not help poor Eibenschütz one whit that he recognized Sameschkin's good-heartedness. On the contrary, he would have much preferred Sameschkin had been a scoundrel. Helplessly and with a feeling of real sorrow he watched how Sameschkin and Euphemia greeted each other. They fell into one another's arms. The large, slender, rust-brown hands of the gypsy held Euphemia's back in a strong and vigorous grip, straining her to him, and Anselm Eibenschütz thought with genuine horror of Euphemia's fine breasts – his by right!

Sameschkin had brought along his appliances on a barrow, as he did every year. The barrow was drawn by a poodle. Sameschkin stowed poodle and barrow in the shed of the hostelry. He established himself in front of the inn, with his oven and his chestnuts. At once the whole place smelled of autumn. It smelled of Sameschkin's sheepskin, of burnt charcoal, and most of all of roasted chestnuts. A haze composed of all these odours floated through the place like a herald announcing Sameschkin's arrival.

An hour later people arrived from Szwaby, to buy roasted chestnuts. A crowd collected round Sameschkin and he sold them chestnuts, roasted and raw. In the centre of the crowd glowed the red coals on which the chestnuts lay. There was no longer any doubt; winter had begun. Winter had begun in Szwaby.

Winter had begun, and with it began the torment of Inspector Eibenschütz.

26

Yes, that was the time when the great torment of Inspector Anselm Eibenschütz began.

'You can't go on living here any more,' Euphemia said to him one night. 'Sameschkin has come, you know!'

'What's Sameschkin to me, what's Sameschkin to you?' he asked.

'Sameschkin,' she said, 'comes every winter. I really belong to him.'

'For your sake,' replied Inspector Eibenschütz, 'I

have given up my home, my wife and the child.' (He dared not say: my child.) 'And now,' he continued, 'you want to get rid of me?'

'It must be so!' she said.

She sat up in the bed. The moon shone piercingly through the round apertures in the window shutters. He regarded her. Never had he so greedily regarded her. In the moonlight she seemed desirable to him, as if he had never before seen her naked. He knew her exactly, every contour of her body, even better than the lineaments of her face.

Why now? he asked himself. Why at all? A great anger against the woman arose in him. But the angrier he became, the more precious she also appeared to him. It was as if his anger made her more alluring every second. He sat bolt upright, grasped her by the shoulders, her body glowed, he pressed her down with enormous force. Thus he held her fast for a while, on the pillow. He knew that he was hurting her, but she did not even groan and that embittered him still more. He threw himself over her, he had the ecstatic feeling that he was destroying her while he loved her. He wanted to hear some sound of pain, he waited for that. She remained still and cold; it was as if he were not sleeping with Euphemia but with a distant image of her. Where was she really? She was already downstairs, lying in Sameschkin's arms. 'Say something,' he entreated her. She was silent, as if to complete his notion that she was only an image. 'Why don't you say anything?' 'I don't know, I've already said everything!' 'Are you really

94

going to live with Sameschkin?' 'I must!' 'Why must you?' 'I don't know.' 'Shall I go away?' 'Yes!' 'Don't you love me?' 'I don't know.' 'Do you love Sameschkin?' 'I belong to him.' 'Why?' 'I don't know.'

She turned away from him. She fell asleep at once. It was as if she had gone on a long journey, without a farewell.

He lay awake and saw the moon through the apertures and felt himself to be meaningless and foolish. His entire life was meaningless. What malicious god had brought him to Euphemia? Soon Inspector Eibenschütz believed that he had gone mad, simply because the words: 'Who really reigns over the world?' formed in his mind. His fear was so great that, as if to forestall it and to carry out his own destiny, he sat up in bed and spoke the sentence 'Who really reigns over the world?' out loud. He was like a man who, out of fear of death, attempts to kill himself, but who goes on living, asking himself: 'Am I really dead? Have I really gone insane?'

He got up very early. Euphemia was still asleep. He gazed at her for a long time, at the sleeping image of the distant Euphemia. She was sleeping with her hands crossed behind her neck in an unusual posture, almost as if she were aware that he was gazing at her.

He washed and shaved with great care, as he did every morning. He was accustomed, from his army days, to concentrate all his thoughts on his face for half an hour in the mornings. He brushed his coat, his waistcoat and his trousers. He moved about very carefully so as not to wake Euphemia. He set to work packing his trunk. But halfway through his task it occurred to him that there would still be things for him to do here. He left the trunk. Out of an official sense of duty, so he thought. He went out on tiptoe.

In the saloon below, Eibenschütz came across Sameschkin, the chestnut-roaster. Sameschkin smiled at him with all his dazzling teeth. He was drinking tea and eating bread and dripping, which he sprinkled with salt as he ate. Poor Eibenschütz felt as if he himself were being sprinkled with salt, and not the bread.

He took a hold of himself and said: 'Good morning, Sameschkin!' At that moment he was filled with a burning hatred for Sameschkin. Then, as he continued to regard him, sitting there garrulous and smiling, he began to hate Euphemia.

He hoped that he would see things more clearly once he had got away.

It was good that the grey was so clever, a clever grey horse. Without him, on his own, Eibenschütz would not have found the way home.

First he drove to the office. For days now, papers had been accumulating there, awaiting him.

He dreaded the papers that were awaiting him.

27

Inspector Eibenschütz stayed at his home for a week in all.

He did not get to see Frau Regina, he sometimes heard the clerk's child screaming.

One day, en route, while he was sitting with Sergeant Slama in the gig – they were travelling to Bloty – he began to talk. His heart was heavy. He had to say something – and far and wide there was no one else, only Sergeant Slama. To whom should one talk? People need to talk to each other.

So the Inspector told the sergeant his story. He related how, until the moment when he had known Euphemia, he had had no idea whatever of the meaning of life. And he also told the sergeant of his wife's deceit with the clerk Josef Nowak.

The gendarmerie sergeant was a very simple man. But he understood everything that Eibenschütz told him, and as a sign that he understood he took off his spiked helmet, as if he could nod with more confidence bareheaded.

Eibenschütz felt quite light at heart after he had related the whole of his story. He became almost cheerful and yet he was so sad.

Sergeant Slama could not think of anything to say, but he knew that it was customary to say something cheerful and so he said, simply and honestly, 'I could not put up with that!'

He wanted to comfort Eibenschütz but he made him

still more sad.

'I too,' began Slama, 'have been betrayed. My wife – confidence for confidence – had an affair with the son of the district governor. She died in childbirth.'

Eibenschütz, who was not affected by any part of the tale, said only: 'Very sad!' He was concerned with his own fate. What was the dead Frau Slama to him?

But the sergeant, once embarked on his narrative and with his heart's wound torn open, continued the tale about his wife. 'There we were,' he said, 'twelve years married. And just think, he was not even a real man, the fellow with whom she betrayed me. He was a youth, the son of the district governor, he was a military cadet.' And, as if this was of special significance, he added after a while: 'A cavalry cadet from Weisskirchen in Moravia.'

Eibenschütz had long ceased to listen. But it did him good that a man was speaking beside him, just as it sometimes does one good when the rain is pouring down, even if one does not understand the language of the rain.

They had only one shop to visit in Bloty, that of the milkman and innkeeper Broczyner, but they stayed there the whole day. Broczyner was found to have five false pound weights in all. Broczyner was reported. Then they went into the inn, kept by the same Broczyner.

The reported Broczyner came to the table and endeavoured to begin a conversation with the Inspector and the sergeant. But both were strict and official, that is to say, they imagined that they were being strict and official.

They stayed there the whole day, till late in the evening. Then Eibenschütz said: 'Let's drive to Szwaby.'

So they drove there.

They played tarock with Kapturak. Kapturak won again and again. Inspector Eibenschütz might also have won if he had only paid attention. But he was thinking of Euphemia and of Konstantin Sameschkin.

At last – it was already well into the night – the two of them came to the table, Euphemia and Sameschkin. Arm-in-arm they came down the stairs. Arm-in-arm they approached the table. They were like brother and sister. Eibenschütz suddenly noticed that they both had the same blue-black hair.

He suddenly felt that he did not desire the woman out of love, as he had done up till now, but out of hate. Sameschkin smiled as always, good-heartedly and with all his white teeth. At the same time he generously extended his large, strong, rust-brown hand. It looked as if he were distributing alms.

He sat down. In his not easily comprehensible speech he announced that business had been good that day. People had come to him from as far as Zlotogrod to buy raw chestnuts.

Euphemia sat between the men. She was silent, she was mute, like a flower which someone has seated at a table rather than placed on it.

Eibenschütz looked at her constantly. He tried to catch her eye at least once, but he did not succeed. Her eyes were wandering somewhere in the distance. God alone knew what she was thinking about!

They resumed their game and Eibenschütz won a number of hands. He was a little shamefaced as he pocketed the money. And still Euphemia sat at the table, a silent flower. She glowed and remained silent.

All around there was the usual noise, caused by the deserters. They crouched on the floor and played cards and threw dice. As soon as they had gambled everything away they began to sing. As usual, they sang the song '*Ja lubyl tibia*', out of tune and with croaking voices.

Finally Euphemia and Sameschkin rose. They went upstairs arm-in-arm and poor Inspector Eibenschütz followed them with his eyes, helplessly. It finally came to him that he must remain here. Yes, remain! He had already drunk a little, had Inspector Eibenschütz. He suddenly felt that he could oust Sameschkin just by remaining here, simply by staying in the hotel. Also he had a dreadful horror of returning home, even though he was certain that he would not see his wife, nor her child, the child of the clerk Nowak. He also felt suddenly very close to Sergeant Slama. Addressing him, Eibenschütz said: 'Tell me, should I stay here?'

The gendarme reflected and touched his head, as if he were once more removing the helmet which he had naturally long since laid aside.

'I think you should stay here,' he said finally, after considerable reflection. And Inspector Eibenschütz stayed on in the border tavern.

Later, a few weeks later, he himself no longer knew why he had asked the gendarmerie sergeant's advice and why he had remained in the border tavern.

All in all, things went very badly for Inspector Eibenschütz at this time. Winter came.

Eibenschütz was afraid of this winter.

28

Ah, what a winter that was! Nothing like it had been seen for years! It arrived suddenly, as a stern and mighty lord might arrive, with whips. The Struminka river froze at once, in a single day. A thick layer of ice covered it suddenly which seemed not to have been formed out of the water itself but to have come from somewhere else, God knows where.

Not only did the sparrows drop dead from the roofs, they also froze in mid-flight. Even the ravens and the crows stayed within close range of human habitations in order to gather just a little warmth. From the first day the icicles hung large and strong from the roofs. And the windows resembled thick crystals.

Oh, how lonely Inspector Eibenschütz felt now! He knew a few souls, Sergeant Slama for example, and the merchant Balaban and little Kapturak. But what did any of them mean to him? In his colossal loneliness the few people he knew appeared to him like lost flies in an icy wilderness. He was very unhappy, was Inspector Eibenschütz. And he no longer sought human company. He felt almost well in his wilderness.

These days he was again living at the inn. He was again living close to Euphemia. He rose very early in order to see her come down. She came down before Sameschkin. Sameschkin did not rise till an hour later. He was good-natured as well as indolent, very indolent. He did not like to get up early, in fact he hated the mornings. Besides, the people who wanted to buy chestnuts came only in the afternoon. What was there for Sameschkin to do in the early morning? He just did not like the early morning.

However, Eibenschütz patiently waited for him too. It did Eibenschütz good to be close to Sameschkin. He even began to love Sameschkin. After all, Sameschkin still held something of Euphemia's sweet, sweet warmth. And it was so cold this winter! And he was so lonely, was Inspector Eibenschütz!

He was so lonely, our Inspector Eibenschütz, that he sometimes stepped in front of the great rust-brown gate of the tavern and stationed himself beside Sameschkin, the chestnut-roaster, careless of his position and his office. Various folk came to buy chestnuts, raw and roasted, and sometimes the Inspector even condescended to sell these people chestnuts, at times when Sameschkin had absented himself. In time Sameschkin became very dear to him. He did not really understand why, but for all that Sameschkin became quite dear to him.

In time he began to love him, as one loves a brother.

29

Everything was going well, or tolerably well, until the day when the improbable happened. It was exactly as if winter had suddenly ceased to be winter. It had simply resolved to be winter no longer. Horrified, the inhabitants of the district heard the ice over the Struminka crack, barely a week after Christmas. According to an old legend that circulated in the neighbourhood, this cracking of the ice signified a great misfortune for the coming summer. Everyone was very alarmed and went about with a troubled face.

Well, they were right. The old legend was right. In fact, a few days after the cracking of the ice a fearful disease began to rage in the town, a disease which otherwise used to appear only during hot summers: it was the cholera.

It thawed in every nook and cranny, one might well have said that spring had already come. At night it rained. It rained softly and uniformly and appeared like a solace from heaven, but it was a false solace. People died off quickly, after barely three days' illness. The doctors said it was the cholera, but people in the neighbourhood maintained that it was the plague. Not that it mattered. Whatever kind of sickness it was, the people died.

As there seemed no end to death, the Governor's office began to send many doctors and drugs to the Zlotogrod District.

But there were many who said that doctors and drugs could only do harm, and that the gubernatorial ordinances were even worse than the plague. The best means of preserving one's life – so they said – was alcohol. And so people began to drink prodigiously. Quite a lot of people who had never been seen there before now came to the border tavern at Szwaby.

Inspector Eibenschütz also began to drink, in immoderate fashion. Not so much because he feared the disease and death, but because the general passion for drink suited him very well. For him it was not so much a matter of escaping the great pestilence as of escaping his own suffering. In fact, it might be said that he actually welcomed the pestilence. For it gave him the opportunity of alleviating his own suffering, which seemed to him so colossal that no pestilence could match it. Actually he yearned for death. The notion that he might be one of the many victims of the cholera was very agreeable to him, even comforting. But how to await death, when one did not know if it would really come, without stupefying oneself?

So Inspector Eibenschütz drank.

All who still remained alive, not to mention the

deserters, became addicted to schnapps. Three of Jadlowker's mortgagees had already been carried off by the cholera and only little Kapturak was left, the indestructible Kapturak. He, too, drank; his yellow wrinkled face did not flush, nothing could have any effect on him, neither the bacilli nor the spirit.

Not everyone died, to be sure, but many were laid up with the sickness.

In the border tavern only the Inspector, Slama the gendarme, the rogue Kapturak and the chestnut-dealer Sameschkin still played. As a matter of fact, one could hardly call him a chestnut-dealer any longer. For he sold virtually no chestnuts these days. How could anyone sell chestnuts in a neighbourhood where the cholera reigned? And reigned with such a vengeance!

People died like flies. Or so the expression goes: in reality most flies die more slowly than men. After three or eight days, according to circumstances, people turned blue. Their tongues hung out of their open mouths. They gave a few more gasps and that was the end of them. Of what use were the doctors and the drugs that had been sent by the Governor's office? One day the military authorities issued orders that the regiment of the Thirty-Fifth was to evacuate the Zlotogrod District immediately and this caused even greater alarm. Until now the poor inhabitants had believed that death was passing through their houses and cottages at random. Now that the garrison was being transferred, however, the government had officially decided and decreed that the 'plague', as they called it, had come to stay. There was no sign that winter was going to return. Everyone longed for the frost which they usually dreaded. But no frost came, no snow came; at most it hailed now and again, and usually it rained. And death went about and reaped and slaughtered.

One day something very strange happened. For a few hours at least, there fell a red rain, a rain of blood, so people said. It was a kind of reddish, very fine, sand. It lay inches deep in the streets and fell from the roofs. It was as if the roofs were bleeding.

People became even more alarmed than they had been earlier by the transfer of the garrison. And although yet another commission was sent to the Zlotogrod District by the Governor's office, and although some learned gentlemen explained to the people in the town-hall that the rain of blood was really a red sand which had come from far away, from the desert, that it was a peculiar phenomenon not unknown to science, this in no way allayed the terrible fear people felt in their hearts. They died even faster and more suddenly than before. They believed that the end of the world had arrived, and who could possibly wish to go on living in such circumstances? The cholera spread with the rapidity of a fire. It spread from cottage to cottage, from village to market-town, from there to the next village. Only isolated farmsteads and the castle of Count Chojnicki remained unaffected.

The border tavern at Szwaby, too, remained un-affected, even though many people passed through its doors. One might almost say that the bacilli met an instant death in the haze of alcohol which hung around the inn.

However, as far as Inspector Eibenschütz was concerned, it was not fear of the epidemic that was driving him to drink. Far from it; he drank not because he was afraid of death but because he had to go on living, living without Euphemia. He had not set eyes on her for some time. Kapturak and Sameschkin between them looked after the shop. Anyway, only a few customers came. Heaven alone knew what Euphemia was doing in her room, alone for days on end. What could she possibly be doing?

One night, after he had drunk a lot, mixing mead and ninety-degree schnapps, the Inspector, in his confused state, decided to go to her room. Was it not his room as well? He could not stand it any longer. The more confused his thoughts became, the clearer the image of Euphemia rose before his eyes. He could almost have grasped her, her naked body, with his hands as she lay there before him. I only want to touch her, he thought to himself, only to touch her! None of the delights her body contains. Only to touch, to touch!

'To touch! To touch!' he said aloud to himself as he stumbled up the stairs. The door was open; he entered. Euphemia had her back turned to him. She was sitting in the semi-darkness looking out of the window. What could she be looking at out there? It was raining, as it did every day. Whatever was she looking for beyond those windows, in the gloomy night, in the rain? A tiny naphtha lamp was burning. It stood high up on the wardrobe. It reminded Eibenschütz of a dim and foolish star. Why did she not turn round? Had he entered so quietly? He was unable to recall how he had entered, or when he could have done so. Although he was swaying, he felt quite steady. He had been standing there like that forever.

'Euphemia!' he cried.

She turned round, she stood up at once, she came to him. She put her arms round his neck, rubbed her cheek against his and said: 'Don't kiss me! Don't kiss me!' She released him again. 'It's sad, isn't it!' she said. Her arms hung limply by her body, two wounded wings. At this moment she appeared to Eibenschütz like a big, beautiful, wounded bird. He wanted to tell her that she was dearer to him than anything else in the world and that he would die for her. But he only said, against his will: 'I'm not afaid of the cholera! I'm not afraid of the cholera!' And yet he had so many beautiful tender words in his heart for Euphemia. But his tongue did not obey. It did not obey.

He suddenly felt dizzy and leaned against the door. At that moment it was pushed open and Eibenschütz fell to the ground. He was aware of everything that took place. He saw exactly how Sameschkin entered and stopped for a second, taken aback; then he heard how Sameschkin asked in his cheerful bawling voice: 'What's he doing here?' and how Euphemia answered: 'You can see for yourself! He's made a mistake, he's tight.'

I'm tight then, thought Inspector Eibenschütz. He felt

someone lift him by the arms – not Sameschkin, these were strong arms – and drag him out through the door which still remained half-open. He felt them let go and he distinctly heard Sameschkin wish him a good night.

That really is a good night, he thought. And he fell asleep, like a dog, right outside the door of his beloved Euphemia, next to Sameschkin's boots.

30

In the morning, very early, the servant Onufrij woke him. He had a letter for the Inspector, a letter with an official stamp. Inspector Eibenschütz got up from the cold hard boards, bruised and tired as he was. He was a little embarrassed in front of the servant Onufrij because he had spent the night there, on Euphemia's threshold. He got up and read the letter with the official stamp. The letter had been despatched by the district medical officer, Doctor Kiniower, and read as follows:

'Dear Inspector, it is my duty to inform you that your child died last night. Your wife's life is in danger. In my opinion she will not survive the night.

Yours respectfully, Doctor Kiniower.'

The letter, barely legible, had been hurriedly written on a prescription sheet in a medical hand. However, it deeply affected Inspector Eibenschütz.

He asked for his horse to be harnessed; he drove home.

He found his wife in bed, in the same bed in which he had always slept with her. Now it was surrounded with medicines of all kinds and there was a smell of camphor, stupefying and unnerving. She recognized him at once. She was completely altered. She had a bluish look and her lips were almost violet. He clearly remembered those lips when they had been red as cherries and had kissed him. He was not afraid of the disease. Why should he fear death? But his wife was frightened to give him her hand, a limp and yellow hand; several times it stretched itself towards him as if she had no will of her own. Once the woman said, evidently with a great and final effort: 'Husband, I have always loved you. Must I die?' It shattered the Inspector that she addressed him not by his name but only as 'husband'. And he had no idea why this affected him so.

The dead child had long since been taken from the room, the woman did not even know it was dead. A nun sat motionless at the foot of the bed, holding a rosary with a cross in her hand. She was as still as an icon; only her lips moved, and from time to time she raised her hand and touched the cross. Eibenschütz sat at the head of the bed. He envied the nun her immobility. He had to stand up repeatedly, take a few steps, go to the window and look out into the wet gloom. He would have liked to do something good for his wife. To make music, for

110

example. As a boy he had once played the violin. Sometimes a shudder went through the body of the dying woman. The whole wide bed shivered and creaked. Sometimes she sat bold upright, looking like a dead candle in her straight white jacket. After a little while she slumped back again, more like an overturned object than a human being.

The doctor came. He could do nothing more. He could only report that the one hospital in the entire district had long been full to bursting. The sick were lying on the floor. The recently stricken had to be left in their homes. He smelled pungently of camphor and iodoform. He moved about in a cloud of stench.

He left. And it became very lonely in the room. The nun suddenly stood up to straighten the pillows, and this seemed like a great event. Then she immediately sat down again and froze into immobility. The rain sang softly on the window-sill. Sometimes one could also hear the sound of heavy wheels outside. The two municipal freight wagons were rolling past, piled high with corpses and covered in black. The drivers wore black hoods, the rain-moist black glistened, and although it was still day the lanterns at the back of the wagons had been lit. They gleamed dimly and swung and tossed; one could almost hear them vibrate although this was only an illusion because of the heavy wheels. The heavy horses wore a festoon of surprisingly delicate little bells, which whimpered softly. Occasionally the half-open wagon passed by the parsonage. In there the priest sat with the Holy of Holies. The lame old horse jogged slowly along, one could clearly hear the wheels crunching in the sticky mud. Once in a while a pedestrian hurried by, canopied by an umbrella. This, too, resembled a tightly stretched shroud. In the room the clock ticked, the woman breathed, the nun whispered.

When the evening began to grow dark the sister lit a candle. It stood there, solitary, improbably large and solitary in the centre of the room, in the centre of the round table. It shed a late and kindly light. To the Inspector it appeared to be the only kind thing in the world. Suddenly the woman raised herself. She stretched out both arms towards the man and fell back immediately with a shrill cry.

The sister bent over her. She touched the cross and closed the eyes of the dead woman.

Eibenschütz wanted to approach more closely but the nun motioned him back. She knelt down. Her black garment and white coif all of a sudden looked very powerful. She called to mind a black house with a snow-covered roof, and this house separated Eibenschütz from his dead wife. He pressed his forehead against the cool windowpane and began to sob violently.

He wanted to blow his nose, looked for his handkerchief, did not find it but grasped instead the flask that he had carried with him constantly for weeks now, pulled it out and took a deep swallow.

His sobbing stopped immediately. He went quietly outside, without hat or coat, and stood there in the foul, putrescent, drizzling rain. It was as if a quagmire were raining down.

31

Things went from bad to worse. It was already early February. And still the pestilence did not let up. Three undertakers died. The municipal employees refused to enter the houses of the dead. A directive came from the Governor's office to employ convicts as undertakers.

The convicts were brought from the great prison in Zloczow to the Zlotogrod District. They were fastened together in batches of six with chains, with long chains, and they climbed into the train clanking and clattering, escorted by gendarmes with fixed bayonets.

They were posted throughout the Zlotogrod District, six in each hamlet and twelve in the little town. They were fitted out with special coats with hoods, all treated with chloroform. In these ochre-coloured and extremely frightening-looking smocks, clanking and clattering and watched over by the gendarmes, they entered the houses and cottages and, clanking and clattering, carried out the coffins and loaded them onto the large rack-wagons of the municipality. They slept on the floor in the gendarmerie guardrooms.

Some of them managed to fall sick with the cholera. They were taken to hospital and gave the appearance of being ill. But in reality they were not ill at all. Many of them even succeeded in apparently dying. That is, Kapturak induced the municipal clerks to record false deaths. In reality, only a single convict died and he was old and had been ill for some time. The clever ones got away. All the others stayed alive. It was as if the chains and the yearning for freedom protected them from the epidemic more effectively than the precautionary measures of the district medical officer, Doctor Kiniower. Even the deserters who came from Russia did not catch it. What avail have such tiny bacilli against such a great human yearning for freedom?

Among the convicts who came from Zloczow jail at that time was Leibusch Jadlowker. He too collapsed one day, just like that, as he was accompanying the hearse. He was released from the chain. Guarded by the gendarmes, he dragged himself along very slowly to the Zlotogrod hospital. Little Kapturak happened to come along the road, as if by chance. Jadlowker amused himself by collapsing for a second time. Kapturak put down his umbrella and he and the gendarme got Jadlowker onto his feet again. Kapturak took his umbrella in one hand and put his other arm under Jadlowker's arm. The gendarme brought up the rear. Kapturak did not need to say anything. He conveyed his intentions to the sick man by rapid glances and by exerting clearly modulated kinds of pressure with his arm. Where shall we take you? asked the pressing arm. – Very risky, answered Jadlowker's arm muscle. – We'll see, everything can be arranged, replied Kapturak's arm, a comforting arm.

Thus they slowly dragged themselves to the hospital. At the entrance Jadlowker was passed a bottle of ninety-degree schnapps. He concealed it quickly and safely.

32

Jadlowker's situation was a very difficult one and
Kapturak racked his brains about ways and means of
managing his death. He was too well-known in the
neighbourhood as the owner of the border tavern and,
besides, simply as Jadlowker. Sergeant Slama knew him
and so did Inspector Eibenschütz. But by a happy
chance Sergeant Slama was transferred to Podgorce as a
result of the application he had submitted at the
outbreak of the cholera. He had been made a staff-
sergeant and commandant of a gendarmerie post.

This would rid them of one enemy at least, but there
still remained the other: Eibenschütz. Jadlowker and
Kapturak resolved to exterminate Inspector Eibenschütz. How was this to be done?

The most important thing was to hide Jadlowker.
One of the cholera patients in the hospital died after
three days; he was the peasant Michael Chomnik,
whom nobody cared about. Nobody cared two hoots
about him and he was buried under the name of
Leibusch Jadlowker, age forty-two, occupation innkeeper, place of birth Kolomea. Incidentally, even these
statements were false. Jadlowker's name was not
Jadlowker, he was not forty-two years old, and he had
not been born in Kolomea.

Jadlowker was discharged from the hospital as cured,
under the name of Michael Chomnik. But where to
shelter him?

For a start, Kapturak collected him at the hospital

gate and took him home for the time being. He had a garrulous wife whom he did not trust, whom he hated in fact. So he said to her: 'A new guest has arrived! My dear cousin Hudes. He will have to stay here a few days.'

Good! Who wouldn't go out of his way for a cousin? Even in times like these? Six chairs were moved together, three a side, and made into a bed for the false Hudes.

He did not stir out of the house. He slept long and ate heartily. Kapturak had only one room and a kitchen. They ate in the kitchen. Although he slept on only six chairs, the false cousin Hudes seemed to fill the entire room. The chairs were never put away. As soon as he had finished his meal, cousin Hudes went into the room to lie down. He fell asleep at once, satiated and unquestioning and strong as he was. He snored and the walls seemed to shake.

What was to be done with him? Kapturak waited for the transfer of gendarmerie sergeant Slama.

This came about in the first days of February; Slama had only a few days left before his departure. Conscientious as he was, he went everywhere, despite the cholera, to take his leave, even of people he would gladly have arrested. He first betook himself to the border tavern to say goodbye to Inspector Eibenschütz. And he was startled when he saw the Inspector again. Eibenschütz was transformed. Eibenschütz was plain drunk. Nevertheless, they drank another two or three small glasses together and said a heartfelt farewell to one another. The Inspector wept a little. The sergeant felt a powerful emotion.

Little Kapturak was sitting close by and pulled out his handkerchief and wiped his eyes. They were dry eyes. He was thinking only of how he could hide Jadlowker. Before the sergeant left he went up to him and whispered: 'Did you know that Jadlowker has died of the cholera? Don't tell Euphemia! Now the hotel belongs to us mortgagees!'

'I'm still in charge here, despite the cholera,' said the Inspector. And Sergeant Slama fastened his cloak, buckled on his sabre, clapped on his helmet and pressed the Inspector's hand once more. 'So, Jadlowker is dead then!' he said with some solemnity. It was as if he were also saying farewell to the supposed dead. Kapturak he only saluted, with two fingers. Then he was gone. Inspector Eibenschütz felt as if he had been abandoned by God and the world. At this moment he yearned for Sameschkin. But Sameschkin was sleeping upstairs with his beloved, his dearly beloved, Euphemia.

33

On the twenty-first of February exactly, a severe frost suddenly arrived and everyone greeted it joyfully.

God in his wrath and in his mercy sends both cholera

and frost, as the case may be. After the cholera the people welcomed the frost.

The Struminka froze overnight. The rain suddenly ceased. The mud in the middle of the street turned hard and dry like glass, grey cloudy glass, and out of a clear glassy sky the sun shone, very bright but also very remote. The drizzle, the last traces of the rain, froze on the wooden sidewalks; and people walked about with iron-tipped sticks so as not to slip. An icy wind blew: not from north or south, east or west, but a wind that seemed to come from no direction at all. Rather, it came from the sky. It blew down from above, just as rain or snow usually fall from above.

The cholera too died overnight. The sick recovered and no one else fell sick. The dead were forgotten, as the dead are always forgotten. They are buried. They are mourned. In the end they are forgotten.

Life resumed its sway in the Zlotogrod District.

Life resumed its sway in the Zlotogrod District, but Inspector Eibenschütz did not care whether the cholera ruled or not. Since his wife's death he had been drinking, not because he feared death, but because he longed for it.

He surpassed all other drinkers. He was once more living in the border tavern at Szwaby; his house in Zlotogrod was managed by the maid and he did not bother himself about how she managed it. He could no longer be bothered about anything.

He drank. He fell into alcohol as into an abyss, into a soft, alluring, feather-bedded abyss. He who had always been so diligently concerned about his appearance, for official reasons that had meanwhile become second nature to him, now began to neglect himself: in the way he carried himself, the way he walked, the way he looked. It began by his lying down on his bed after a whole night of drinking without taking off more than his coat, his waistcoat and his shoes. He undid his braces but was too lazy to remove trousers and socks. From his barrack days he had been in the habit of washing and shaving at night before going to sleep, as duties began early at six o'clock the next morning. Now he began to postpone shaving until the morning. But by the time he got up it was late, around noon, and he remembered that many people shaved, or were shaved, only every other day. He still had the strength to wash himself. He still inspected himself in the mirror, not so much to see how well he looked but rather to discover whether he was still looking passable. Very often, after he had got up, he was overcome by the unpleasant desire to give his tongue a close inspection, although he was not at all interested in it. And as soon as he had once stretched out his tongue at himself, out of obstinate curiosity as it were, he could not help making all sorts of grimaces in front of the mirror; and sometimes he even called out a few furious words at his mirror image. At times he found it almost impossible to break away from this self-contemplation in the mirror, and then he would reach for the bottle, which always stood at the foot of the bed. He poured a slug in the water-glass and then another and another. After he had had three such mouthfuls it

119

seemed to him that he was once more the old Inspector Anselm Eibenschütz. In reality he was nothing of the kind. He was an entirely new, entirely different Anselm Eibenschütz.

Every day, in the early morning, he had been in the habit of drinking hot tea with milk. But suddenly one night it occurred to him that he could not drink tea with milk as long as Sameschkin was here and it was not possible for him to be together with Euphemia. Not until the spring . . . not until the spring! he cried out to himself. And he began, every morning, to pour the tea they brought him up to his room into the washing-bowl. For he was ashamed, and he did not want anyone to notice, that he no longer had a hot drink in the morning. Instead of the hot drink he took a mouthful of ninety-degree schnapps.

He immediately felt warm and well and in spite of everything life looked cheerful. He felt very strong and believed that he could overcome all obstacles. At this moment he, Inspector Eibenschütz, was very strong and the chestnut-roaster Sameschkin would soon disappear.

In uniform or out of it, Eibenschütz had always paid great attention to his trouser-creases. Now, however, since he slept in his trousers, trouser-creases seemed not only superfluous to him, but downright repugnant. Equally superfluous and repugnant was the idea of leaving his boots in front of the door to be cleaned.

For all that, Inspector Eibenschütz still appeared imposing to everyone and only a few people were able to perceive any change in him. Except perhaps Sameschkin who said to him one morning in all his artless good nature: 'You have a great, a colossal sorrow, Herr Eibenschütz.'

He stood up and left without a word.

34

Poor Eibenschütz soon had to acknowledge to himself that remarkable things were happening to his brain. He noticed, for example, that he was losing his memory for quite recent events. He no longer knew what he had done, said or eaten the previous day. He went rapidly downhill, our imposing Inspector. He had to pretend, when he came into the office and the clerk discussed with him an order he had given the previous day, that he remembered everything perfectly. And he gathered every ounce of shrewdness he possessed just to drag out of the clerk what he might have said the day before.

Outwardly he still appeared imposing, did Inspector Eibenschütz. He was still a young man, thirty-six years old in all.

He still held himself bold and erect, on foot and in the gig. But within him burned the schnapps when he had drunk it, and the longing for it when he had not yet drunk it. In reality there burned within him the yearning for another person, any person, and a longing akin to homesickness for Euphemia. Her picture was firmly lodged in his heart; at times he had the feeling that he need only open up his breast and reach inside to draw the picture out. And he did in fact contemplate the idea that one day he might open up his breast.

Other strange changes also took place within him at that time: he noted them, he even regretted them, but he could no longer become his old self again. He would gladly have done so; in fact it could be said that he yearned even more for his old self than he did for other human beings.

He became increasingly inflexible and unrelenting in his official duties, for which the new sergeant who had taken Slama's place, namely Sergeant Piotrak, was also somewhat to blame. He was redheaded, and he confirmed the truth of the old folk superstition that redheads are malicious. Even his eyes, though they were bright blue, gleamed in a slightly reddish way, inflamed and burning at the same time. He did not speak so much as growl. When he entered a shop it was only with reluctance that he put down his rifle, as the law decreed. He seldom laughed, but was forever telling the Inspector tedious stories in a solemn manner. When they entered a shop together in order to check the weights and measures he did not have to open his mouth. Inspector Eibenschütz felt his gaze, and this sharp blue and, at the same time, reddish gaze fell with deadly accuracy on the most suspicious object. One day the gendarmerie sergeant Piotrak happened to discover that they were also entitled to check the quality of the wares, and the Inspector obeyed him. He asked to see the wares. He found rotten herrings and watered schnapps and linoleum gnawed by mice and damp matches that would not burn and materials eaten by moths and Samogonka, the home-distilled schnapps made by poor peasants, brought across from Russia. It had never occurred to him that it was one of the duties of an Inspector of Weights and Measures to check the wares as well, and the gendarme Piotrak, who had drawn his attention to it, acquired a special importance.

Very gradually, very insidiously, Inspector Eibenshütz slid into a certain dependence on the gendarme; he did not acknowledge this to himself but he felt it, and sometimes he even experienced a fear of the redheaded man. Especially frightening was the fact that the gendarme was quite abstemious. He was always sober, and he was always malicious. His short, thick fists were covered with reddish hairs, looking like the spines of a hedgehog. This man not only carried the regulation weapons. He was himself a weapon.

Sometimes he would take a smoked-ham sandwich out of his large black service bag, break it in two in the middle, and offer half to Inspector Eibenschütz. Although he was hungry, Eibenschütz would take it with some reluctance. Sometimes he had the notion that a few of the reddish bristles which grew in such profusion on the backs of Piotrak's hands had also fallen on the butter or the ham.

At the same time he also felt that he himself had become a malicious person and that Piotrak was not really all that much worse than he was. He took the flat bottle out of his back trouser-pocket and gave a good hearty swallow. Thereupon it seemed to him that he was not malicious at all, that he had to be strict, that he was only doing his duty – and that was that! Boldly, and filled with a certain frantic gaiety, he entered the shops, the large, the medium-sized, the small and the tiny ones. Sometimes the few customers fled, for they were afraid of the gendarmerie, of the authorities, of the law in general. The gendarme drew out from his service bag the longish, black, official notebook, bound in silk rep. His pencil at the ready resembled his bayonet.

Inspector Eibenschütz stood behind the counter and the merchant beside him seemed stunted and shrivelled (one must imagine a shrivelled nought beside some terrible numeral) and Eibenschütz dictated to the gendarme: 'Grammes!' or: 'Three pounds,' or: 'Six kilos,' or else: 'Two metres'. He set down the false weights before him as one might set down chessmen. Standing there at his full height, he felt very powerful, the arm of the law. The gendarme recorded, the merchant trembled. Sometimes his wife would come out from the room at the back of the shop and would wring her hands.

Everyone asked themselves why the cholera had not attacked Inspector Eibenschütz. For he raged worse than the cholera. Through him the coral-dealer Nissen Piczenik went to prison, also the draper Tortschiner, the milkman Kipura, the fishmonger Gorokin, the poultry-dealer Czaczkes, and many others.

124

Like the cholera he raged in the land, did Inspector Eibenschütz. Then he returned home, that is, to the border tavern at Szwaby, and drank.

It sometimes happened during one of his terrible official visits, that the wife and children of a tradesman would throw themselves on their knees before him and implore him not to make a report. They would cling to his fur. They would not let him go. But the red-haired Piotrak stood immobile beside him. No wife, no children dared approach him because he was in uniform. Eibenschütz would say: Why not let him go? Whom has he ever harmed? They all rob one another in these parts. Let him go, Eibenschütz! But it was the old, the former Eibenschütz who spoke thus. The new Eibenschütz said: The law is the law and there stands Sergeant Piotrak and I myself was a soldier for twelve years, and what's more, I myself am very unhappy. And my heart is not in my job. And all the time Piotrak seemed to nod assent with his red head to everything the new Eibenschütz said.

35

At the end of February Eibenschütz received notification of the decease of the convict Leibusch Jadlowker, the supervision of whom had for certain reasons been entrusted to the Inspector.

On the evening of the same day, as if he had known, Kapturak reappeared at the inn after a long interval. He made the usual obeisance and sat down at the table at which Eibenschütz, Sameschkin, Euphemia and the new sergeant Piotrak were sitting.

Everyone played tarock, Kapturak lost. For all this, he was inordinately cheerful.

It was not clear why. Besides the usual stupid expressions and meaningless phrases which tarock players employ he uttered new, freshly invented and even more meaningless ones, such as: 'The pig has wind!' or: 'I'm losing my braces' – or even: 'Dung is gold' and more in a similar vein. In the middle of these expressions and as he sat there, appearing to reflect tensely which card to play next, he said, as if absentmindedly and in the tone of voice in which he had just been repeating his nonsensical phrases: 'Herr Inspector, so things have worked out for you? Your enemy is dead?' 'What enemy?' asked Eibenschütz. 'Jadlowker!' And at the same moment Kapturak laid a card on the table. 'He was one of the cholera convicts,' he continued, 'and he caught it. He's been rotting under the ground for months. His worms have stuffed themselves by now.' Euphemia said: 'It's not true;' she turned very pale. 'Yes, it is true!' said Eibenschütz, 'I have the official report.' Euphemia rose, without a word. She went upstairs to weep. Sameschkin was the first to lay down his cards and the only one to say: 'I'm not playing any more!' Even the red-haired gendarme Piotrak put his cards down; Kapturak alone went on as

126

if he were playing against himself. Then, abruptly, he too laid down his cards as if he had made a sudden decision and said: 'Then we mortgagees shall inherit this inn, that makes six of us.' And he looked at the Inspector.

It had grown very quiet at the table, the good Sameschkin could hardly bear it. He got up and went to the music-box at the bar, to throw in a dreier. The music-box immediately began to spew out the Rákóczy March in a splendid blare of brass. Through the blustering noise Kapturak said to the gendarme: 'You know, since you've been here our Inspector has become very strict. All the tradesmen curse him and three have already lost their licence on his account.' 'I do my duty,' said Eibenschütz. And he thought of Euphemia and of the old Eibenschütz he had once been, and of his dead wife, and especially of Euphemia, yes, he thought especially of Euphemia and that he was now truly a forsaken man in a forsaken neighbourhood.

'You don't always do your duty,' said Kapturak very quietly. But at that moment the music-box had stopped blustering so that even the quiet words rang out very loudly. 'How does it come about that you never inspect a certain shop? You know the one I mean!' Eibenschütz knew well which shop Kapturak had in mind, but he asked: 'Which then?' 'Singer's,' said Kapturak. 'Where's this Singer?' asked the gendarme Piotrak. 'In Zlotogrod, in the centre of Zlotogrod,' replied Kapturak, 'right beside the fishwife Czackes, whose licence you took away three weeks ago!' The gendarme threw a questioning, suspicious glance at Eibenschütz. 'Tomorrow we'll go and have a look!' said the Inspector. Suddenly he felt a great fear of Kapturak as well as of the gendarme. He felt he must have another small glassful.

'Tomorrow we'll go and have a look!' he repeated.

Kapturak gave a wide and soundless smile. His thin lips bared a total of four yellow teeth, two above, two below; they seemed ready to chew up his own smile.

It was true that Inspector Eibenschütz had never yet taken a look at Singer's shop. It was the only one in the district, to be sure. Despite his great honesty and sense of official duty he had quite deliberately refrained from troubling the Singers.

Besides, it was such a miserable shop that it stood out even among the exceedingly miserable shops of the neighbourhood. It did not even have a sign but a common slate, on which Frau Blume Singer renewed her name in chalk every few days, and especially when it had rained and the writing had become illegible. It was a tiny little house; it consisted of one room and a kitchen, and the kitchen also served as the shop. On a tiny rectangle of open ground before the entrance lay a dungheap of moderate size and beside it stood a wooden booth. This was the lavatory of the Singer family. Not far from it, usually on the rubbish heap, which was now covered by a thick crust of snow and ice, the two Singer boys played in the few hours they did not have to devote to study. For they had to study. At least one of them was destined one day to become his father Mendel's heir.

Alas! It was not a question of a material inheritance.

God forbid! It was merely the reputation of a learned and righteous man. In the room behind the kitchen and the shop Mendel Singer studied day and night, between the two beds, each of which was pushed against one of the walls. On the floor, in the middle, lay the straw palliasses of the children.

Mendel Singer had never concerned himself with anything other than holy and pious words and many pupils came to him. He lived wretchedly but he required nothing whatever. Twice a week, on Mondays and Thursdays, he fasted. On ordinary days he took only soup. He slurped it from a wooden dish with a wooden spoon. Only on Friday nights did he eat trout in sauce with horseradish. Everyone in the little town knew him. Twice a day they saw him running to the prayer-house, there and back. He hurried along on thin legs, in white stockings and sandals, which he covered with heavy galoshes in winter. His coat danced in the wind. His heavy fur cap sat low over his eyes, a fringed pelt. His sparse beard waved. The hard prow of his nose thrust against the air, as if it wanted to carve out a path for his face. He saw nothing and no one. He was engrossed and lost in his humility and in his piety, in thoughts of the holy words which he had just read and in joyful anticipation of those yet to be read. Everyone respected him, even the peasants of the neighbourhood came to him when they were in distress, asking for his advice and intercession. Although he appeared never to have seen the world and men, it was nevertheless evident that he understood both the world and men. His advice was excellent and his intercessions helped.

His wife concerned herself with the earthly matters of everyday life. She had scraped together the money for the licence and for the purchase of a goods by begging from the rich and well-to-do people of Zlotogrod. Alas! What goods! One could get onions, milk, cheese, eggs, garlic, dried figs, raisins, almonds, nutmegs and saffron. But how minute were the quantities and how frightful was the condition of these provisions! Everything was in a muddle in the small, dark-blue, lime-washed kitchen. It looked as if the childen were playing at being shopkeepers. The small sack holding the onions and the garlic rested on the large bucket which contained the sour milk. Raisins and almonds stood in little heaps on the cream cheese, separated by greaseproof paper from what was underneath. Beside the two cream jars crouched the two yellow cats, guardian lions of a kind. In the middle, a pair of large rusty scales hung down from the ceiling on a black wooden hook. And the weights stood on the window-sill.

The kind of people who might have been poor enough to have shopped at Blume Singer's did not exist in the neighbourhood. And yet they still managed to live, despite everything – for God helps the poor. He bestows a little compassion on the rich, so that from time to time one of them comes and buys something which he does not need and which he will throw away in the street.

36

This, then, was the shop which Inspector Eibenschütz
invaded the following morning, together with the
gendarme Piotrak. Although a severe frost prevailed, a
good dozen people nevertheless collected in front of the
shop and the children ran out from the Jewish school
opposite. It was about eight in the morning and Mendel
Singer emerged from the prayer-house. When he saw
the assembly before the little house he was alarmed, for
he feared his house was burning. Some of the curious ran
up to him and cried: 'The gendarme has come! The
Inspector has come!' He rushed inside. And he was even
more alarmed than he would have been by a fire. A real
gendarme with a rifle stood there while Eibenschütz
checked the goods, the scales and the weights. The two
cats had disappeared.

The cream was sour, the milk curdled, the cheese
wormy, the onions rotten, the raisins mouldy, the figs
withered, the scales unsteady and the weights false. Now
it came to official procedure. Everything must be written
down. When the gendarme pulled out his big official
black calico notebook, Mendel Singer and his wife felt as
if he were drawing the most dangerous of all his
dangerous weapons against them both. The Inspector
dictated and the red-haired gendarme wrote. A fire
would have been a bagatelle.

The penalty amounted to exactly two gulden and
seventy-five kreuzer. The business was not to be
continued until the fine had been settled. The purchase

of new scales and new weights cost a further three gulden. Where is a Mendel Singer to find two gulden seventy-five and a further three? God is very kind but he does not concern himself with such trivial amounts.

Mendel Singer reflected on all this. That is why he went up to the Inspector, took off his fur cap and said: 'Your Excellency, Herr General, I beg you, strike everything out. As you can see, I have a wife and children!'

Eibenschütz saw the lean raised hands, the meagre bony cheeks, the poor sparse beard and the black, moist, imploring eyes. He wanted to say something. He wanted, for example, to say: 'It's no good, old chap, it's the law.' He even wanted to say: 'I hate this law and myself into the bargain.' But he said nothing. Why did he not say anything? Because God had closed his mouth and the gendarme was pushing Mendel Singer away. One glance from him was enough. One glance from him was like a fist. And off they went, with weights, scales and the black book.

If Frau Mendel sold anything more today, be it only a single almond, she would be locked up for four months.

The few onlookers and the children who had loitered outside ran off.

'We shouldn't have done that!' said Eibenschütz to Piotrak. 'In spite of it all he's an honest man!'

'No one is honest!' said the gendarme Piotrak, 'and the law's the law.' But even the gendarme was not entirely happy.

They drove to the office and deposited the articles

with the clerk and they both felt that they needed a drink. Good! So they drove to Litwak's inn.

It was Wednesday that day and market day in Zlotogrod, so the inn was full of peasants, Jews, cattle-dealers and horse-copers. When the Inspector and the gendarme sat down at the great table at which a good two dozen people were already squatting beside each other on smoothly scrubbed benches, a suspicious muttering and whispering arose. Then people began to speak louder and someone mentioned the name of Mendel Singer.

At that moment a thickset, broad-shouldered, heavily-bearded man got up from the bench opposite. In a great arch he spat across the table, across all the glasses and, with masterly accuracy of aim, right into the Inspector's glass. 'There's more where that came from!' he cried and a great tumult arose. Everyone got up from the benches and Eibenschütz and the gendarme tried to climb over the table. They reached the door, but at that moment the broad-shouldered, bearded man had already pushed it open. For a short time they still saw him running along on the white snow-covered road. He ran very fast, a dark stooping streak on the white snow, towards the pine forest that fringed both sides of the road. He disappeared to the left, as if the forest had swallowed him up.

It was afternoon, it was already beginning to get dark. The snow was taking on a light bluish tinge.

'We'll get him alright,' said the gendarme.

They turned back.

133

The gendarme Piotrak was really very uneasy about it. Had he not been wearing his full equipment and his heavy winter boots, as prescribed by regulations, he might well have been able to pursue the light-footed one. However, he was certain that he would find him and deal with him in the end, and that was some comfort. Probably he was a dangerous criminal. One would hope that he was a dangerous criminal.

The gendarme Piotrak questioned everyone in the tavern but not a single person chose to know the miscreant. 'He's not from this neighbourhood!' they said.

However, Eibenschütz had the feeling that he had already seen the man somewhere. He did not know where and when. Night prevailed inside his poor head and there was no sign of dawn. He drank to lighten the darkness but it only grew darker. All around he sensed a great animosity among all the people, as never before.

They got up eventually, climbed onto the sleigh and drove to Szwaby. 'Kapturak will know who it was,' said the gendarme on the way.

The Inspector could not think of anything to say. After a while he said: 'It's all the same to me!'

'Not to me!' said the obstinate Piotrak.

37

Jadlowker had been sitting in Kapturak's house for several weeks now. He could not stand it, so he made an excursion. He thought that on a market day in Zlotogrod he would not encounter any acquaintances, not even in Litwak's inn. Would you believe it! Along came the new gendarme and his old enemy, Eibenschütz. It was thoughtless, even careless, to attract attention by spitting.

He took a very roundabout way to get back to Kapturak's house from the forest into which he had fled. The frost was severe; fortunately one could risk walking over the bogs. He waited in the forest until night had completely set in. Then he marched southwards, along the whole length of the curve which the marshes formed round the little town. The frost was certainly a blessing but he was horribly cold. His whole body felt stung and scourged. In the short fur coat Jadlowker was wearing he froze just as much as if he had been dressed only in a shirt.

It was already far into the night when he reached Kapturak's house. Now the fear which he had suppressed with all his might on the way began to fill him with redoubled strength: namely, the fear that the gendarme might already be there, waiting for him. He decided to tap very softly on the window shutter. He breathed a sigh of reflief when he saw Kapturak step outside. Kapturak beckoned him in. A new fear gripped him: could one trust even Kapturak? – But whom else?

135

he presently said to himself, and he came closer.

They went in. Kapturak sent his wife out into the kitchen. 'Sit down, Jadlowker,' said Kapturak. 'What are you up to? Do you want to destroy yourself and me as well? Are you a grown man? Are you a youth? Are you playing pranks? Schoolboy pranks?'

'I couldn't help myself,' said Jadlowker.

'You were probably recognized,' said Kapturak. 'I heard all about it afterwards from Litwak. I knew at once it was you. Naturally, I didn't show any sign. What are you going to do now?'

The half-frozen and perplexed Jadlowker – his ears burned like red lamps on both sides – said: 'I don't know!'

'I've decided,' declared Kapturak, 'to shut you up. You'll be better off here with me than in Zloczow jail.'

Where does one hide an endangered guest? Inexperienced people hide him in the cellar. And that is a mistake. If there's a house search, the first place the gendarmes go to is the cellar. No one can escape from a cellar. Experienced people, on the other hand, shut up an endangered guest in the attic. That is where the gendarmes go last of all. Besides, it is easier to hear what is going on from up there. Thirdly, there is a skylight. One has fresh air and one can make a quick getaway.

So Jadlowker mounted the steep ladder that led to the attic. A chair and a palliasse, a bottle of schnapps and a jug of water were also allotted to him.

Kapturak wished him goodnight, promised to bring him food regularly, and went away. As a precaution he slipped the bolt which was fixed to the trap-door of the attic. When he had climbed down the ladder he stood there for a while and reflected. He reflected whether he should take the ladder away or not. And he finally decided to take it away. He carried it into the yard and leaned it against the roof. He had made up his mind to use only the skylight when passing Jadlowker his food.

It was cold in the attic, colder even than in the cell, and Jadlowker tore open the palliasse at the top end and slid right down into the sack and put his fur coat over his head. Through the open skylight, which did not shut, the clear frosty night shimmered bluish-white. Before he fell asleep he noticed the motionless bats which were hibernating all around on the washing-lines above his head. For the first time in his life the lawless Jadlowker was afraid. And this fear was enough to send him into a deep, though restless, sleep.

He awoke early in the morning; the bitter breath of the icy morning woke him. He crept out of his sack with difficulty, took a swallow from the flask, put on his fur coat and went to the skylight. Flocks of crows recently woken from their sleep circled round the roofs, looking as if they were flying only in order to warm themselves. He saw the red sun rise, it looked like an orange, and at the sight of it he felt hungry. He knew he would have to wait for a good two hours before Kapturak would arrive with his food. He listened at the trapdoor, for a good two hours he was occupied with nothing else than his hunger. It was as if his hunger were an affair of the head and not of the stomach. At last Kapturak appeared with

137

tea and bread, not at the door, however, but at the skylight. He passed everything through very slowly; on the short journey up the ladder the tea had already grown cold, so severe was the frost. Jadlowker ate and drank hastily. He asked only, 'Anything new?' 'Not yet,' answered Kapturak, climbed down the ladder again, and placed it a little to one side.

After Jadlowker had satisfied his hunger other thoughts and feelings began to preoccupy him. Suddenly and without knowing why he thought of the fine carp and pike which he used to sell at the fish-market on Thursdays. He was occupied by the thought that, in order to kill them, he had grasped them by the tail and dashed them against a kerbstone and this made him remember that one destroys men by doing the reverse. One takes a stone – which can also be a sugar-loaf – and dashes it against a man's head. Strange thoughts come to one when one is shut up in an attic. One remembers, for example, that one has enemies in the world and that the greatest of them all is Inspector Eibenschütz, the source of all ill and Euphemia's lover into the bargain. Sameschkin is her lover, too, but that's another story. Sameschkin has old tribal rights, and besides, he is not an official. And further, he has not sent Jadlowker to jail. If there were no Eibenschütz one could live in peace. Sameschkin will go away in the spring. Sergeant Slama has been transferred. Who will recognize Jadlowker with a fair beard? A lot of strangers come to this district! And one's name isn't really Jadlowker at all. One has already changed one's name once before! One has already

grasped fish by the tail and struck them against the
kerbstone. It's done the other way round with men. One
takes a sugar-loaf and strikes them on the head from
behind. But where? But when? Eibenschütz is not there
at night, in Odessa harbour.

If Eibenschütz did not exist, one could live in peace.
But he does exist. He must not be allowed to exist any
longer, he must not be allowed to exist any longer,
thinks Jadlowker. He must not be allowed to exist any
longer! He thinks of it all the time. The crows sometimes
settle near the skylight. Jadlowker throws them some
crumbs. He sits and freezes and waits for the spring, for
freedom and for revenge.

38

One day something strange happened: head forester
Stepaniuk found a hanged man in the border forest. He
was cold, blue and rigid when he was cut down. The
district medical officer, Dr Kiniower, said that he had
already been dead for several days, that he had hanged
himself about a week earlier. Nobody knew who he was
and the gendarme Piotrak notified the examining
magistrate. The latter came from Zlotogrod. He had the
corpse taken to the mortuary there. The inhabitants of
the entire district were summoned, a dozen at a time, on

specific days, to identify the dead man. There would have been no need to summon them. They poured in from all over, out of curiosity alone. Even Sameschkin, although he was not summoned because he did not belong to the district, went along out of curiosity. But he alone recognized the dead man: it was the horse-minder Michael Klajka. He had been locked up two years before. He had been one of the convicts chosen to deal with the removal of the corpses of the cholera patients. And the fact that he had died in hospital, of the cholera, and been buried on a certain day, had been recorded in the books and given the official stamp.

Well? Had he risen from the dead in order to hang himself in the border forest? An investigation was instituted. Some convicts, who were brought from the prison, also recognized their fellow prisoner, Michael Klajka. It only took a week before two of the district clerks were arrested and confessed that they had been bribed and had made out false death certificates. They also confessed that it was Kapturak who had bribed them.

Another week went by. The outcome of the investigation was conveyed to gendarmerie sergeant Piotrak and to Inspector Eibenschütz, and they were given the task of continuing to meet Kapturak in the border tavern as before. So they continued to meet him and they played tarock. He felt quite safe. He knew nothing of the arrest of the two district clerks, and the money the relatives of the 'dead' convicts had paid him had long been safely on the other side of the border, with the money-changer

Piczemk.

A few day later, quite early in the morning, shortly after he had taken Jadlowker his breakfast up the ladder, he heard a familiar ringing of bells, the bells of a sleigh. The sleigh stopped, the ringing trembled on a while longer, there was no doubt that the sleigh had stopped in front of his gate. He had a sense of foreboding, what was a sleigh doing in front of his house so early in the morning? He opened the shutters. In the sleigh sat the gendarme Piotrak and Inspector Eiben-schütz. He had no time left to remove the ladder. He reflected rapidly that it would be better to run outside at once and welcome the terrifying guests. So he ran outside, calling as he ran, 'What a surprise! What a surprise!'

The two of them climbed down and Eibenschütz said: 'We wanted to pay you a short visit. It's still too early, Litwak is still closed. We'll only stay a quarter of an hour, if we may, just long enough to drink a schnapps and some tea. You've got that, eh?' Kapturak no longer had any doubt that they had come because they suspected him of harbouring someone, or at least of hiding something suspicious. He said: 'I'll go and fetch the schnapps,' and he left the room and quickly scrambled up the ladder. 'They're here,' he called through the skylight. Going down he no longer skipped onto the individual rungs but slid down both struts of the ladder using his hands and thighs. He ran into the kitchen to fetch the schnapps. He re-entered the room cheerfully with the bottle and three glasses.

'Do you have a cellar?' asked the gendarme Piotrak.

'Yes,' said Kapturak, 'but I haven't fetched the schnapps from the cellar. It's too cold in the cellar.'

'Where did you fetch it from then?' asked Piotrak.

'From the attic,' said Kapturak and smiled. It was as if he had made a joke and was apologizing at the same time for having made it.

The red-haired gendarme actually took it for a joke and laughed. Kapturak slapped his thigh and doubled up. He joined in the laughter, out of humility rather than conceit. The gendarme and the Inspector emptied their glasses and got up. 'Thanks for the hospitality,' they said as with one voice. They climbed back on the sleigh; Kapturak accompanied them. He noted that they glided off in the direction of Pozloty.

When they had disappeared from sight he took the ladder out of the yard and put it back in the hall. He had decided to send Jadlowker away, he had a presentiment of evil. Nimbly he climbed up, opened the trap door and went in. He saw Jadlowker walking restlessly up and down, between the washing-lines hung with bats. 'Sit down!' said Kapturak, 'we must talk!' Jadlowker knew at once what was up. 'So I must go,' he said, 'but where?' 'Where? That's just what we've got to think about!' replied Kapturak. 'It looks as if you're not going to be counted among the dead any more, hence this unexpected visit to my house. I'm sorry, but I have to send you away. You must admit that I've treated you like my own child, even though I'm your mortgagee. And I haven't taken a penny from you!' 'Where shall I go?' asked Jadlowker. He was sitting on the chair in his fur coat, freezing. Through the small round skylight, which looked like a ship's porthole, the frost stormed in, a grey wolf, a raging, hungry grey wolf. It was dark, even though the sun was shining outside. But the relentless, ice-blue sky sent only a meagre light through the round skylight into the attic. Up above there prevailed a kind of frosty blue half-darkness. Both men looked pale.

Where? Where? That was the question. 'I set all the others free,' said Kapturak, 'and let them run where they wished. It was probably a mistake. I should probably have kept them together. But as for you – I don't know what's best. I think it's best for you to go back to Szwaby, to go home. Who's to recognize you there? Euphemia won't betray you and Sameschkin is a blockhead, he won't recognize you. That still leaves Eibenschütz! Of course, Eibenschütz!' 'What's to be done with him, then?' asked Jadlowker. He got up. He could not possibly remain seated where Eibenschütz was concerned.

Kapturak, who had been standing still throughout, began to walk to and fro. It looked as if he wanted to get warm but in reality he was not freezing at all, he was actually feeling hot from too much reflection. For a long time he had been harbouring the thought that the world would be a better place if Eibenschütz were not there.

'Eibenschütz must go,' he said – and remained standing.

'How so?' asked Jadlowker.

'Sugar-loaf!' said Kapturak – that was all. He remained standing for a while. Then he said: 'We're going to drive over, tonight. Sugar-loaf!' he repeated. 'I'll fetch you, Jadlowker!'

Before he left the attic Kapturak made a sign with both hands. It looked as if he were holding a sugar-loaf in his hands and was beating someone over the head with it.

Leibusch Jadlowker nodded.

39

In the evening they rode out to Szwaby on the sleigh, Kapturak and Jadlowker. Jadlowker wrapped himself in a sheepskin coat with a high collar so that no one would recognize him.

It was already pitch-dark when they arrived and drove in through the wide, open gate of the border tavern. Jadlowker knocked on the back gate, the high-arched gate, painted red, which gave onto the road. Kapturak went straight into the inn.

There were only a few guests that day, being a Tuesday. It took a long time before Onufrij heard the knocking and went out to open the back gate.

'It's me,' said Jadlowker, 'let me in quickly. Is the gendarme there?'

'Come in, sir,' said Onufrij, who had no idea that Leibusch Jadlowker belonged to the dead. 'Have you escaped from prison?'

'Yes, get a move on!' said Jadlowker, and then, as they neared the lamp, 'Will I be recognized?'

'Only by your voice, sir!' said Onufrij.

'Where's Euphemia?' asked Jadlowker.

'Still in the shop!' whispered Onufrij. 'And Sam-eschkin's standing outside the shop with his chestnuts.'

'Good,' said Jadlowker. 'Go inside!'

The dog, Pavel by name, welcomed Jadlowker, joyfully sniffing up at him with raised muzzle and wagging tail. 'Don't bark! Don't yell!' Jadlowker whispered to him. The dog jumped up at him, quietly and silently, and licked his hands.

Jadlowker first looked in through the windows which gave on to the yard. The inn was almost empty. He had not forgotten, on the way, to climb out of the sleigh when he and Kapturak were driving by the frozen Struminka, and to dig out of the snow one of the large angular stones which were to be found there in abundance. This stone he now tied in his handkerchief.

He stepped back from the window and lay in wait by the gate. He was filled with a monstrous, irresistible lust to kill. He no longer thought of the real purpose of the murder but only of the murder itself. He gave no thought at all to his own safety but only to the killing. A great wave of voluptuousness, of hate and lust to kill, went through his heart. Everything was without pity in this night and in this world. The stars that stood in the sky that night were strange, cold and made of silver, a frosty, almost spiteful silver. From time to time Jadlowker looked up. That day he hated the sky and the stars. And in prison he had yearned for them so!

Why did he, Jadlowker, hate the sky today? Did he believe that God sat up there, behind the stars? Perhaps he believed it but he would not admit it. Over and over again, over and over again, a voice within him said: God is there. God can see you. God knows what you intend to do. But another voice within him answered: God is not there, the sky is empty, and the stars are cold and remote and terrible, and you can do what you will.

And so Jadlowker waited for the familiar ringing of the sleigh that belonged to the hated Eibenschütz. Round his wrist, his right wrist, he had tied the corners of the handkerchief in which the stone had been wrapped. He waited. Eibenschütz would come.

40

Indeed, Eibenschütz did arrive half an hour later, unfortunately accompanied by the gendarme Piotrak. Jadlowker, who had thought that the Inspector would come alone, realized at once that he could achieve nothing. At first he hid in the shadow of the barn which bordered the yard opposite the gate, and waited. When he saw that

146

the Inspector let the gendarme go ahead and was unharnessing the grey himself, his heart trembled with rapturous, murderous hope. And soon after, the Inspector approached the stable in order to tie the grey to the big iron ring that was fastened to the stable door.

While Eibenschütz was tying up the grey, Jadlowker rushed out of the stable. Eibenschütz was about to utter a cry, but he fell down at once and the cry died in his throat. Jadlowker struck the forehead of his enemy, the Inspector, with the handkerchief in which the angular stone was wrapped. Eibenschütz fell to the ground with a mighty and terrifying crash. He was a heavy man; Jadlowker had not expected him to be heavy. The grey had not yet been properly tied up, the knot came loose, and the nag began to wander through the yard with reins trailing. First, Jadlowker bent over Inspector Eibenschütz. He was cold and dead, gave no gasp. Then Jadlowker got hold of the horse and tied it fast to the iron ring of the stable door. Then he crept into the barn.

Two hours passed before Sergeant Piotrak came outside to look for Eibenschütz. He found the Inspector in front of the barn, seemingly lifeless, so the gendarme called the groom Onufrij and the two of them dragged the heavy corpse to the sleigh. Onufrij fetched ropes, they secured the motionless man firmly. He lay right across the tiny sleigh. The grey was harnessed, the gendarme took the reins and drove to Zlotogrod, straight to the hospital.

To be sure, Sergeant Piotrak believed that he was driving a dead man, that the Inspector, whom he had

147

come across by the stable and the barn, had suddenly had a stroke. But this was not so. True, the Inspector was beginning to die, but he was still alive. How could he, poor Eibenschütz, know that he had been hit on the head with a stone? How could he know that he had been tied to the sleigh with ropes? While he was being taken for dead he was experiencing something quite different:

He was no longer an Inspector of Weights and Measures, he was himself a trader. He had nothing but false weights, a thousand, ten thousand, false weights. He was standing there behind a shop counter, the ten thousand false weights in front of him. The counter could not hold them all. And at any moment the Inspector might come.

Suddenly there was a ring – the door had a bell – and in came the Great Inspector, the greatest of all Inspectors – so it seemed to Eibenschütz. The Great Inspector looked a little like the Jew Mendel Singer, and also a little like Sameschkin. Eibenschütz said: 'But I know you!' But the Great Inspector replied: 'It's all the same to me. Duty is duty! Now we shall test your weights!'

Good, you can test the weights now, Inspector Eibenschütz said to himself. They are false, but what can I do about it? I am a tradesman, like all the other tradesmen in Zlotogrod. I sell with false weights.

Behind the Great Inspector stood a gendarme with plumed helmet and bayonet and him Eibenschütz did not know at all. But he was afraid of him, his bayonet glittered so. The Great Inspector began to check the weights. Finally he said – and Eibenschütz was extremely surprised: 'All your weights are false, and yet they are all correct. So we shall not report you! We believe that all your weights are correct. I am the Great Inspector.'

At that moment the gendarme arrived at the Zlotogrod hospital. The Inspector was unloaded, and when the duty doctor arrived he paused for a moment and then said to the gendarme Piotrak: 'The man is dead! Why have you bothered to bring him here?'

41

So died the Inspector of Weights and Measures, Anselm Eibenschütz; and, as they say, no one cared two hoots about it.

Sergeant Piotrak succeeded in establishing that Jadlowker had killed the Inspector. Kapturak, after he had been arrested, and after a stringent cross-examination, spoke of a grudge Jadlowker had towards Eibenschütz.

By chance, two more so-called cholera victims were caught, namely the pickpocket Kaniuk and the horse-thief Kiewen. Kapturak and Jadlowker had already been held in the Zloczow remand prison for eight days when the great annual event of the Zlotogrod District suddenly occurred. That is, the ice over the Struminka broke and spring began.

The chestnut-roaster Sameschkin packed his things: first the sacks, then the oven, then the rest of his wares, with the chestnuts in a special leather sack.

Before his departure he said to Euphemia: 'It's a desolate spot, this border. Will you come away with me for ever?'

Euphemia, however, thought of all kinds of possibilities in the tavern, and more besides. 'Until next year,' she said. But Sameschkin no longer believed her. He was not as stupid as he might appear to people. He had his suspicions and he silently resolved never to return to that venomous neighbourhood again.

It was a magnificent spring day when he drove off. The oven stood on his cart. The loose sacks were tied round his shoulders. The larks trilled high in the heavens and the frogs croaked just as merrily in the marshes. And so the good Sameschkin went on his way, minding his own business. What did all this actually have to do with him?

I shall never come here again, he said to himself. And he had the feeling that the larks and the frogs concurred.